ALL THE BEARS SING

All the Bears Sing

stories

Harold Macy

HARBOUR PUBLISHING

Copyright © 2022 Harold Macy

1 2 3 4 5 — 26 25 24 23 22

All rights reserved. No part of this publication may be reproduced, stored in a retrieval system or transmitted, in any form or by any means, without prior permission of the publisher or, in the case of photocopying or other reprographic copying, a licence from Access Copyright, www.accesscopyright.ca, 1-800-893-5777, info@accesscopyright.ca.

Harbour Publishing Co. Ltd.
P.O. Box 219, Madeira Park, BC, VON 2H0
www.harbourpublishing.com

Edited by Pam Robertson
Cover design by Libris Simas Ferraz / Onça Design
Text design by Carleton Wilson

Printed and bound in Canada
100% recycled paper

"A Heartbreak of Winter Swans" appeared on CBC Radio One's *Rewind* (2016) and in Harold Macy's book *The Four Storey Forest: As Grow the Trees, So Too The Heart* (2011).
"Gelignite" appeared in *PRISM International* (Spring 2014).
"Lipstick" appeared in *Rhubarb* (2015).
"The Sweet-Talking Ladies in the White Trailer" appeared under a different title in *The Malahat Review* (Winter 2017).
An earlier version of "Unclipped" won first prize in the North Island College 3-Hour Fiction contest (2013).

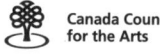

Canada Council for the Arts   Conseil des Arts du Canada   Canadä

BRITISH COLUMBIA ARTS COUNCIL   BRITISH COLUMBIA
Supported by the Province of British Columbia

Harbour Publishing acknowledges the support of the Canada Council for the Arts, the Government of Canada, and the Province of British Columbia through the BC Arts Council.

LIBRARY AND ARCHIVES CANADA CATALOGUING IN PUBLICATION

Title: All the bears sing : stories / Harold Macy.
Names: Macy, Harold, 1946- author.
Identifiers: Canadiana (print) 20220242917 | Canadiana (ebook) 20220242933 |
    ISBN 9781990776007 (softcover) | ISBN 9781990776014 (EPUB)
Classification: LCC PS8626.A29 A75 2022 | DDC C813/.6—dc23

Whenever I'd pull on my boots and head for the truck, a wet nose, unconditional love and wagging tail accompanied me. Watchful, ever vigilant and welcome company: *Meggie, Comet, Clancy, Duffy, Conrad.*

And family dogs still among us:
Jackson, Finnegan, Cooper, Frankie.

CONTENTS

The Sweet-Talking Ladies in the White Trailer 11
Stir the Still Waters 14
Downhill 19
A Heartbreak of Winter Swans 27
Gelignite 30
Buses Come, Buses Go 38
Unclipped 46
Into the Silverthrone Caldera 56
Delta Charlie 68
The Patient Soil 72
Little Habits 74
Nightingale 78
Buried on Page Five 84
House, Waving Goodbye 87
Ditch Clothes 96
Beyond Yuquot 103
Donkey Shame 105
All the Bears Sing 116
Lipstick 121
Overburdened 123
Ephraim 171
By the Book 180
The Beast Within 191

Acknowledgements 203
About the Author 205

Outside of a book, a dog is man's best friend.
Inside of a dog, it's too dark to read.

—Groucho Marx (attributed)

THE SWEET-TALKING LADIES IN THE WHITE TRAILER

The early summer lightning storms frolicked a hellish two-step across the forested steeps of North Island, trailing fire from Wolf River up to the hemlock-balsam jungle of the Artlish that has rarely felt this devil's lick. The unusual drought earlier in the season parched the forests into cornflakes and shrivelled the needles and twigs. Lower branches curled down in search of scant water; underfoot, moss and lichen crumbled to grey lifeless powder, and the earth lay hollow in its thirst. Then, this swath of thunderbolts. Big fires around Gold River, above Muchalat Lake along the power line's umbilical, an angry swarm close to Vernon Camp and blustery Atluck Lake.

So I'm pounding my kidneys to mush while driving a stiff-sprung, unforgiving sonovabitch of a two-ton Forest Service flat deck over the logging roads of the Island's spine, bringing hoses, pumps, drinking water, Gatorade, relay tanks, fittings, food, foam, gaskets and gas to the exhausted crews. It's thirty-seven degrees C air temp on the fire line—add another ten from the dragon's breath. Dust, ash, smoke. Just being here is like a two-pack-a-day habit. Hours of dragging hose uphill, setting up containment systems, digging fire breaks, then the fickle wind veers and balls of burning debris jump the line and suddenly you have fire in front, fire behind. *Run, boys, run.* Not just boys. Most crews have women as members or leaders. Boot camp grads or seasoned vets, they have muscles in their black snot.

But I am too old for that and just drive the truck, thank God. A bit of pump duty—keeping the four screaming Wajax Mark 3s running flat out pushing water uphill, and cleaning the intakes of swamp goo from the pond we're rapidly draining. And like Sisyphus, on this blistering bug-bit afternoon, it seems an unending if not outright audacious act—wildfire control—but we do it.

The Antler Lake fire burned to a scant kilometre from Gold River. Tourists in the SuperValu parking lot set up lawn chairs in front of their tethered RVs to point up at the helis bucketing water endlessly onto the roaring head of the firestorm. When it hit the crisp slash in a logged-off block, the beast rejoiced and tore off uphill faster than a man could ever run. The high-voltage power lines to Port Hardy were at risk. The air was so full of carbon and fried squirrels, fire already arcing from one wire to another, showering sparks onto the ground, torching off even more.

Orders flow from Quinsam Fire Base. There is mutual aid from the other provinces and the NWT—specialists in fuel behaviour, incident management and fire weather. There are a couple of hotshot unit crews like the Port Alberni Thunderbirds, each with distinctive grimy uniforms and earned pride. Word comes in: the crews at Muchalat Fire 1098 need a long list of supplies. We scurry about the warehouse filling totes and boxes, strapping down pallets of fuel, grabbing a detailed map of the lacework of forestry roads—one driver, one navigator. Out the gate and do a radio check.

Beside the base is a white trailer full of angels. The twenty-metre aerial is our mother watching over us, reminding us to make contact every two hours, thanking us when we do, gently chiding when we don't. The door to the lair is plainly marked "Do Not Enter." At any one time the two or three women will be tracking a half-dozen helicopters, several airplanes and ten fire line crews, as well as those of us bouncing over the washboard, baby heads and potholes toward the black mountainsides. They remain serene, with voices of menthol—oral oases in a parched and smoking desert where the red dirt is baked like pottery. I have never walked over to the trailer to put a face to these calming voices nor has any of the crew—we prefer to build images from our own need.

One day rolls into the next—the air tastes metallic. Everyone is walking around like zombies. Crews rotate through, bringing fresh blood for the fiery kraken. Though we pray for rain, the sky cannot be trusted, the clouds only bring more fire, and we greet them with red-eyed suspicion. We have few friends these days.

STIR THE STILL WATERS

My best friend and I were strutting the one street of our coastal village, on the lookout for adolescent fun, usually at someone else's expense. Ahead of us was our latest target. Impossible for us to ignore since we had lived here all our lives and knew absolutely everything about everybody; the adults knew nothing and people from outside knew least of all. As if our world was the only one that mattered, the only one that would ever matter.

At the mercy of teenage juices, I was beginning to think about things beyond my squeaky voice and grander than girlfriends. Things less easy to define, things I didn't have the question for let alone the answer. Like doubt. Like belief.

"See that one there? The weirdo!"

The guy wore a red toque with lots of curly blond hair rolling out from under the rough-knit seams. He had on common wool trousers and a canvas Carhartt jacket, frayed at the cuffs but bulged up strangely over his shoulders. I thought I saw a ripple under the cloth, which made me wonder what a hump is made of anyway. Muscle? Fat? I pictured a mound of boneless flab, like fleshy Jell-O, that sorta churned my stomach.

"Hey, hunchback, lose your bell tower?"

"Yeah, get a haircut, hippy!"

The guy turned and gave me this little grin, a cousin of a smile but with an odd look of disappointment and hope that made my heart drop. Sarcasm, my usual response, fell short. He didn't say anything, just smiled and kept walking. Kenny and I glanced at each other, laughed thinly at the unexpected response and continued on our harmless hunt.

I worked part-time at my mom's diner on the hill up from the wharf where the fishboats moored. It was no fancy joint, just your basic caffeine, suet and starch. Had the early shift, opening up in the first light before school and on weekends.

Our community was small enough with few surprises, so the back kitchen door of the café was left unlocked except during tourist season, when some of the upscale refugees from the city showed up in their big plastic boats that looked like giant bleach bottles. Others arrived from the city to open the handcrafted, though vulnerable, glass and cedar doors on expensive waterfront cottages overlooking private coves. That's when strangers, with their urban expectations, broke into our lives. I thought this guy was one of them, just ahead of schedule.

The next morning, when I banged through the swinging half-doors with the round windows into the dining room, the guy we'd been mocking the day before was already in a booth, the one at the window where you could see who was going or coming on the docks. I was surprised, him just sitting there in the dim light. Only it wasn't all that dark around him. Kind of a glow I didn't really notice at the time. I thought he was just backlit by the sunrise in the front windows because it disappeared when I switched on the row of flickering fluorescent overheads and the buzzing red neon "Open" sign and everything looked normal.

Nothing peculiar, other than that. He ordered the Big Breakfast Platter—bacon, brown toast, three eggs over easy, side of hash browns, pair of pancakes and a pickle. No coffee, just water. Sat there bent over the table with yolk dribbling off his chin.

Every time I passed by, he'd look up with storm-grey eyes, tilt his head a little bit like an invitation and give that slight grin, as if we were supposed to be sharing a private joke or a secret. By now the regulars were filling the booths and round chrome counter stools, cocky loggers waiting for the crummy to take them into the hills, and bachelor fishermen who lived in seclusion on their stinky trollers and gillnetters. Though I managed with simple orders from the grill, I was always relieved when Mom came in to take over in the kitchen. Orders stacked up and I was kept running.

When I went to clean the table where the guy had been, it was empty and a twenty was tucked under the plate—a big tip for an eight-buck breakfast—and he was nowhere to be seen, not in the diner, not walking down the sidewalk. There was a funny lingering smell. Not the usual rotten salmon from the cannery, more a sharp chemical tang like kelp left under the sun by the high tide.

Just up the hill, the school bell rang. I yelled to Mom I was leaving, grabbed my knapsack and headed out the front door. A few doors up from the diner was the fisherman's supply store, the front window hung with every colour of lures, hootchies, flashers and painted plugs with brutal triple hooks. On the shelf below them was a spread of sharp gutting knives, wool socks, rolls of line and fingerless gloves.

Old Mr. Marinillo shuffled out with a box of gear, got in his decrepit salt-rusted pickup and started to nose down the steep slope toward the wharf and his boat, squinting behind thick glasses nearly opaque with a widower's grime—still mourning his Gabriella, gone two years now. From the steps of the diner I could see into the cab and I waved.

Suddenly his mouth made an open hole in panic, baring yellow teeth as the truck picked up speed. He glared at his feet as he rolled past. I could see his leg pumping the brake pedal with no effect. Other fishermen leapt out of the way as the truck barrelled down the hill onto the rough boards of the wharf, slammed over the bumper logs and tumbled into the bay. I joined the mob running across the dock to gather at the edge. We saw the truck lying on its side, driver's door deep in the silt and garbage, leaking gas and oil making a rainbow swirl on the surface—yellow, violet and maroon, like a fresh bruise—prettier than a catastrophe ever should be.

All these valiant men of the sea stood helpless, none of them good swimmers, only looking at each other, waiting for someone to dive the six metres down to the truck. Silent. Just staring, no one doing anything. No heroes.

I remembered some old rope piled behind the freight shed at the shore end of the dock, so I dropped my knapsack and ran. At the back of the building lay the rope, but also a pile of clothes that looked familiar—tan jacket, wool pants, red toque. I thought I heard another splash. I grabbed the coil and raced back to the edge of the dock to peer into the water, now nearly opaque with oil from the truck.

Through the sheen I thought I saw a figure swimming into the deep shadow and I swear to this day it had wings, not fins or flippers, stroking down and down to where it yanked open the side door, pulled out a limp Mr. Marinillo, and pushed him to the surface. Then it turned and disappeared into the depths.

One of the fishermen finally tied the rope around his waist, handed off the other end, jumped into the water, and grabbed the bobbing old man. Three men on the dock hauled them both up. Mr. Marinillo lay coughing and puking up the pancakes I'd set in front of him not a half hour before. He'd left without paying,

"Put it on my tab. I'll settle up later," he had said over his shoulder.

"He barely got his door open," someone remarked. "Lucky, eh?" They thought the old fisherman did it all by himself. No one said anything about the diver or the wings. I kept quiet and just stared at the water.

I heard the ambulance coming from the mission hospital, so I picked up my pack and walked shakily around the freight shed toward school. The pile of clothes lay there, still undisturbed. I looked around for the man who'd left the big tip then glanced up at the overcast sky, corrugated like the tin walls of the net loft. Something moved through the clouds, churning them around.

No fireballs and lightning, no balance of the earthly and the divine; just a stirring of the still waters, just an angel pressing his ancient heart to mine.

DOWNHILL

Sam stood for a moment at the top of the hill above the cop shop and the donut store, then stooped to tie his shoes tighter, tucked in his shirt, turned the grimy ball cap backwards, swallowed another swig of courage, and with a deep breath, pushed off.

The hill had seemed longer when Sam ascended it just after dawn that day. On the way up, he had scanned the paved shoulder for potholes and windrows of gravel from the street sweeper, and for the shattered shards from a tossed bottle. Broken glass insulted him. Such a waste. His own load was firmly packed with care.

He wasn't sitting in a car, isolated from such obstacles and cushioned by tons of steel and plastic, but instead was hunkered over a chrome shopping cart pinched from a local grocery store. It was full of bottles and cans from his day's collection in the upscale neighbourhood at the top of the hill—the one with gold-painted fire hydrants. *Oh, to be a dog.* That thought had kept him amused and grinning as he rummaged through the curbside blue boxes, ignoring the stares from the expansive bay windows.

With the first shove of his foot, the cart began to rattle and roll. This was no ordinary cart. While many of his peers stole a new one each day and ditched the old behind the bottle depot for someone else to return for two bits, his was customized for his ongoing use. A cement block was bungee-corded onto the lower rack for stability at speed. He had duct-taped a set of bicycle handbrakes to the side rails of the basket and, helped by the guys with their soul patches and piercings at the bike shop near the bridge, screwed brake arms and pads over the back wheels of the cart. It was a brilliant, though yet untested, invention and just one more reason to stay out of the Sally Ann shelter, where someone would be sure to steal it. Besides, who needed the noisy, smelly shelter, with all its rules, bunk beds and weirdos, when it was full-on summer?

But this wasn't just for fun. It wasn't for the thrill of speed like a kid with a new wagon. Sam had a task. Besides delivering the cargo clinking and rattling in the cart and collecting his day's earnings, he yearned to see Li Chu, who ran the bottle depot.

Li, her uncle and aunt, her five-year-old son Henry and seven-year-old daughter Amanda all lived upstairs. When Sam was out in the evenings, he looked up at their warm and inviting steamed-up windows. There were red paper lanterns with golden dragons twisting around them.

Before Li Chu opened her depot, the buyers operated out of garages and cube vans. Sly and devious, they used many tricks to cheat Sam and the other collectors, moving from one location to another, always owing money to the binners.

"The bastards would figure up the bottles, they'd say this type or that had no refund, and then they'd keep them and sell them. I may be a drunk, but I can count and add," he once confided in Li Chu. "You don't do that. You treat us well." Us. The feral fraternity of misfits like Sam who scuttled out from their havens each day to sift the town's detritus for value.

The do-gooders hounded them like summer horseflies. Always the give and take game: we'll give you rent and food money if you sign up for the rehab program. The only ones he trusted were the nurses in the van that made the rounds of the squats and campsites. They didn't make moral judgements. They just washed the feet that stayed too long in soiled socks.

Sam had lived his adolescent years in a small mountain town where the deep snowpack drove desperate elk into the streets and alleys, ignoring the scrawny dogs that had their own winter issues, like frozen ears and frostbitten tails. The people stayed housebound and the drinking started young. He was the life of the party, always had jokes to make everyone laugh; he could imitate all the pop stars and had a stock of tricks to keep the mood rolling. His friends started smoking pot but he didn't like the foggy feeling. Some sought solace in the plunge of a needle but that made him shiver. Beer was preferable—until he discovered the cheaper and heavier kick from wine and sherry, and then there was no going back and little to go back for. Short-term jobs in logging and construction gave him money but no roots.

One day last April, he was in the cavernous depot unloading his bottles. Li's two children peered around the counter at him. He caught their eyes and winked. Sam picked up three beer bottles and began to juggle them expertly, catching each one by its long brown neck. The children stared open-mouthed then giggled and clapped their small hands. Emboldened by the attention, Sam tossed the bottles higher and higher until they almost touched the high ceiling, tumbling and spinning in the air. He never missed a one. Henry and Amanda were spellbound and wanted more.

He waved them over to the counter where he was sorting. Without a word, he began stacking beer and pop cans into a pyramid on the floor. He worked quickly and motioned them to bring him more cans from his cart. Excited to be a part of the fun, they laughed and ran back and forth with arms full, and the tower grew taller than them, then taller than Sam. Now even he was enthusiastic and pulled over a stool to stack them even higher. Other binners stood around and shouted encouragement. Sam felt like a star. With each can, the whole structure trembled. Now there remained but one left to place at the very pinnacle. Amanda stared up wide-eyed with a red pop can in her hand. Sam stepped down from the stool.

"You do it. I'll hold you up." And he hoisted her on his shoulders.

They carefully ascended and she delicately set it in place. Suddenly a flash filled the room, and Sam turned his head to see Li Chu behind the counter, lowering her camera. She beamed with an ear-to-ear grin. Henry hopped up and down, pointing at his sister atop the man on the stool. Sam gently lowered Amanda from her perch. He wanted this moment to last forever—the applause, the warmth of the little girl in his arms, the cheerful expression on Li's face.

"I guess everything better get back where it belongs, eh?" he said.

Li's eyes sparkled when she looked intently at him. She turned and said something to her son in a language Sam could not understand. The boy's eyes widened in surprise and question. Li nodded. Henry ran off to the back room and returned with an old grocery cart left behind by another binner, looking once more at his mother, who nodded again, then at Sam, who stood to one side with Amanda still clinging to him, in no particular hurry to get down. Henry yelled in a high squeaky voice and charged the pyramid with the cart. The racket was deafening and satisfying. The crowd erupted in a chorus of cheers.

When the noise died down, Li came up to Sam and quietly spoke.

"You bring me all your bottles and I'll give you a bonus every Saturday. Don't tell anyone else. Just you and me, OK? Sam, you hearing me? OK?"

"Why's that?"

"Lots of guys come here. Most of them steal the blue sorting trays and I gotta buy new ones. You don't do that. You come real regular and don't bring any junk. I think you a good guy. That's why. OK?" She paused and looked at the mountain of cans. "You made my kids laugh. Me, too. Not enough of that here. Too much work all the time. You good man for that, Sam."

Sorting rancid bottles ten hours a day was not what Li Chu had imagined when she moved from Taiwan to Canada. Her teaching certificate was not accepted here so her options were suddenly limited.

She met other Chinese who had coarse, menial jobs—in the forest tangle picking salal for the florists, digging clams and oysters on the mud flats while racing the midnight tides.

Four years, she figured, and she could sell the business and turn to the local college for upgrading. Each night she ran tired fingers over the abacus and clacked her progress one bright bead at a time. Often during the workday, when the stream of returnables seemed never-ending, she dreamed of a treasure in the bottom of a bottle—a gold bracelet or a misplaced diamond ring.

She knew her English was passable—teaching ESL assured that—but when she stood in a checkout line of blond, blue-eyed people, she felt alone and conspicuous. Sidelong glances from adults, undisguised staring from children emphasized her foreignness.

But now there was Sam, his attention to her kids, his kind eyes and soft voice. But she knew his first fondness. Him with his bottle, her with her dreams. People change, though.

Knee-deep in cans, Sam was elated by the attention, but saddened because he knew that sooner or later, it too would tumble with a clatter; he would do something stupid and lose that glow. That was what kept him at the bottle; it was dependable and trustworthy. He knew the routine.

After cleaning up the mound of cans and delivering his loaded trays to the counter, the ritual was the same. Li handed him the money with a concerned look on her round face. He wadded the cash into a ball and stuffed it in his jeans, nodded politely to her and the kids and headed for the liquor store two blocks away, where he bought the shining bottle that reflected his sharp need. He was hardly out the door before he was twisting off the cap and tossing it in the bushes.

He finished the dive to the bottom of the plonk and settled into the glow of victory. The sun broke through the clouds over the glacier, welcoming him to a familiar half-buzzed condition. He traced his steps back to the depot where he saw Li sitting in the sun, her back against the warm cement blocks, resting from hefting cases of bottles all day, every day. He had the strongest urge to lay his sinewy hands on her and massage her shoulders. Instead, he grinned and hunkered down beside her. The silence was comfortable, almost intimate. He snuck a quick glance, caught her perfect smile and shivered despite the sunshine.

The cart picked up speed and he lay lower over the jingling collection of bottles and cans. The road swooped and curved to the engineer's arc, flowing like black lava cooled and contained by the curb. At each bend in the road, Sam dragged one shoe to make the curve. Cars honked but he concentrated on the pavement before him. Faster now and his bleary eyes watered, tears running back from the corners.

The little wheels were never designed for speed and they wobbled and shivered like a dog passing peach pits. Sam knew that slowing down was not an option; his brakes, though clever, only hissed discouragingly against the hard rubber. The best he could do was to ride it out, to keep out of the gravel. A police cruiser came up the hill and the baby-faced Mountie stared open-mouthed as they passed each other. Sam dared not turn his head to see if the cop pulled a U-turn and came after him.

The last corner lay ahead, then the traffic lights. Sam dropped his left foot and leaned way out to the side, like the sailboat racers in the magazines at the library.

The cart skidded sideways into the curve; Sam clamped his teeth together.
Bright red lanterns.
Grinning benevolent dragons.
Li Chu.

A HEARTBREAK OF WINTER SWANS

All December, in rosy grey morning and dusky evening, we are blessed with a brassy orchestra passing over our rooftop. The trumpeter swans are aloft with their hoarse two-tone song, but I often wonder if it is a lament or a hosanna. Necks outstretched, they fly with an effortless ease, black legs tucked under snow-white bodies. Arising from the small lakes in the foothills of the Vancouver Island ranges to the west, they head toward the snow-free pastures and corn stubble of our neighbours' dairy farms, or down to the beach to follow the retreating tide, claiming eyebrows of gravel and the feast of rich seaweed, small invertebrates and stranded fish. Their foraging gabble is quieter, more content than that on wing.

But this morning they fly with urgency. Blustery gales with driving rain have kept them grounded for several days. They hunger. Yet even as the Pacific Low moves inland, the wind barely slackens. They flex wings as wide as my outstretched arms to battle the lingering buffets of storm. The racket and frothing from dozens of webbed feet slapping across the ponds is like no other sound in the winter rainforest. Scrambling into the sky they weave just above the thrashing treetops, skidding and side-slipping, tumbling in the unseen gusts, searching for eddies of calmer air like me picking my way down a rocky trail.

They fly at night under the moon and stars, guided by an ancient compass. They fly even when the cloud bellies lie low over the conifer forest. I cannot see them but hear them long before they appear. Wingtip pinions rattling. Always honking. *I am here, where are you?* White birds in a white sky over a white land. Jabbering about what is important to swans.

Social animals, they thrive in community—browsing, resting or flying. They are monogamous and mate for life. This is the heartbreak. The call of a single bird sounds sad, its song more melancholy, more beseeching for companionship. I often count the birds in the flock and when it is an odd number, I wonder who is the loner. Perhaps it is a grey juvenile yet to mate, or having made a foray into romance, was beaten by another darting neck and harsh beak, leaving a wound on the love-struck heart of the hopeful challenger. Maybe it is a hen widowed by accident. Such a large congregate animal has few predators, but collisions with power lines around alluring pastures take a toll. In low light a wingtip brushes the hot wire, an arc sparks, the farm lights dim and a big bird falls from the sky.

Perhaps the loneliness comes on the perilous migration from our wintering estuaries through the rugged Coast Range, riding ridgewind and buoyant thermals in long glides above deep glacial valleys, then north over the Interior plateau as ice melts on the large resting lakes—Chilko, Tatlayoko, Babine and Nechako. Ever on the move toward the ancestral nesting grounds on the northern taiga where wetlands and tussocks of reeds offer refuge for their downy chicks.

How many such flights can one bird make until the powerful breast muscles fail, until the noble heart stutters, so in late summer when the flock arises as one to move on, he can only watch? *Go. You go. Go now.* Does his mate paddle anxiously around him, coaxing, gently prodding until the departing multitude pulls her and her fledglings into movement? Does she make one last circle over his white form on the dark water? Calling, yearning in her wild soul. He shudders and his long neck drops into its own reflection on the lake. A fox vixen watching from the shore notices his strange stillness and waits until he drifts close. Her pups will gorge and prosper on the rich dark meat.

When his mate returns to this island and the familiar cattail pond for winter, is hers the solitary voice I hear mourning?

No other. No other will ever do. I am here. Where are you?

GELIGNITE

After thirty years of marriage to an oaf, one day I hopped in the Chev. Said I was going out for milk. I'd had enough, and the kids were grown. I did like so many women and slipped out the door one morning and drove west, toward the coast, watching the house fade away in the rear-view mirror until I could cover it by holding up my thumb. I didn't tell him I was going; I didn't pee in his shoes like my friend Sally did with her dearly beloved. No note, no nothing—just gone. I bet he's still at home, waiting in his recliner for a supper no one's going to bring.

I grew up on a fruit farm in the Okanagan, the only child of an apple man. Summers picking and hauling totes, sunlight warm on my bare brown arms, a babble of talk as the workers moved through the orchard. Winters pruning the trees, springtime spraying dormant oil and sulfur off the back of the tractor, me learning how to drive on that Ford 9N, bouncing and jerking the clutch—Dad hanging on and waving the spray nozzle like a knight in combat, laughing at my driving and yelling at the unseen enemy. But when the codling moths finally won, he got to daytime drinking in the dark corners of the empty packing shed and things got real ugly.

To this day I can remember hearing the soft flutter of grey wings as the up-valley wind brought the migrating adults, hundreds bumping blindly against the windows of our farmhouse. Dad just standing in the kitchen, staring at his beat-down reflection in the glass. For every bug hitting the panes, there were a thousand in the trees laying their eggs under the bark scales. Some nights in bed waiting for sleep, just around that time between nodding off and staying up to reach for a magazine, everything fuzzy like the grey moths, I could almost feel them crawling on my body. Run. Squash them on the dirt path until it's greasy. Fall down in the slime. Bad dreams.

I was only eighteen when I met Harvey. He was selling agricultural chemicals out of the back of an old rusted-out van. He slept in there while he was on the road and for years after he still smelled of Atrazine and Roundup. Didn't smell it then, though. I smelt adventure and escape so I married him. Standing up in the front of our church in the summer, pregnant by Christmas. What a mistake, but I didn't discover this until well after his ring had worn a furrow round my finger. Still, he did get me out of one kind of valley into another, and gave me two kids that turned out pretty good.

Lordy, he was unpredictable. No more perching on the edge of the sofa when the truck crunched on the driveway gravel, wondering what sort of man's coming through the door. Hoping whatever happens, it doesn't wake the kids again.

Which is why I am pushing so hard now. Close to fifty, I can't afford to take more chances. Don't have the time.

The first night after I left, I ended up in Princeton. Driving into the late afternoon, squinting like a day-caught orchard mole, I blamed the sun for the few streaks down my face. It was summer and full heat reflected from the dry mountainsides.

Thirsty work, leaving your life behind. The Princeton Hotel was a shaky old building that has since burnt to the ground. That evening in June, with a hot, smoky wind coming from the wildfires up the Tulameen, it seemed like a palace to me. I got one of the few rooms they still used and tossed my stuff onto the bed. The squeal of lonely, tired springs told me it wasn't any Sealy like at home. I'd miss that. After a quick shower and a touch-up on the old war paint, I went down to the pub.

From the bright glaring sun to the dark and cool parlour, like jumping into the Similkameen River, which I had done earlier—my hair was still damp. Blinking my eyes to adjust to the dimness, I walked to an empty table and plunked myself into a worn seat, caught the eye of the barmaid, and got my first cold beer. It went down with a satisfying sizzle, slaking the road thirst and beginning to build insulation around my recent sudden departure. The second and third joined it and the buzz crept in.

Tracing my finger through the wet rings left by the glasses, I didn't see him come up.

"Join ya?" A short fireplug of a man stood before me, blue eyes crinkling with his question. Nice teeth.

"Free country." I sat up and waved to a chair. My God, I think I even flipped back my hair and licked my lips glossy as he turned away and ordered two more before dropping solidly into the red vinyl seat.

The beers came and we clinked glasses. I leaned forward to study him. He wore clothes worked in but clean and had a few tattoos colouring up his arms with that bruise-like blue as the ink slowly leached out. Where does it go? Into the blood, through the kidneys, pissed out into some cracked toilet? He had a shaved head, glistening with a sweat sheen on that late summer afternoon. A soul patch dangled from his lower lip. Later I would persuade him to grow a full bushy beard. But I told him you have to let me shave your neck, keep it clean. I always wanted to shave a man. Something about holding a keen, sharp razor just over the jugular vein keeps them honest on a customary basis.

"So, whaddya do for money?" I asked him.

"Professional homewrecker." He smiled and handed me a business card. *David J. McNeil, Licensed Blaster. 'I don't stand behind my work, I stand behind a tree.'* Funny guy. I needed a laugh.

Dave and I spent that summer running around the province blowing stuff up. I learnt a lot about how things are put together by how you take them apart. We went up behind Lillooet, to the old mines of Bralorne. There was this forty-five-metre brick chimney from an abandoned smelter. For years antique hunters and scavengers scraped and dug through the ruins and now the chimney presented a real hazard of coming down on them. Dave thought that would be a just fate. Culture vultures, he called them.

The chimney towered over the abandoned company town. It's the same all across the province. Some big business comes in to dig up or cut down, and once it's all gone the playboys move on, leaving everyone else to make their own way. There were a dozen houses with black vacant windows and kicked-in doors. Some of them half burnt from drunken parties. I wondered about their stories: payday at the mine site, dances in the hall, babies born, men—never to come up from the shafts—mourned.

After putting out his warning signs and stringing up bright ribbon with "Danger—Blasting Zone" all round the site, Dave set to work laying the charges. I saw him glance up once at a row of shacks in the chimney's slim shadow and get a devilish grin. The first charge was placed in a cavity he chiselled out of the bricks with a pickaxe, sweating in the sun but still with that crazy smile. He called me to bring over a handful of what looked like fat sausages from Satan's kitchen. Stacking them in like a Sunday brunch table, the last one he loaded with a safety cap and fuse. He then went all round the chimney placing four more bundles with a delay fuse linking them to the first charge.

When it was all set up, he explained, "The first one, it goes off and takes out a wedge from that side. The chimney leans that way, and then the back ones go five milliseconds later. That keeps it in one piece all the way down, like a tree. Now if I wanted it to crumble all in one pile, they'd all go at once. But I don't wanna do that, so watch this."

He pulled a Bic from his pocket and lit the fuse. Raised on a diet of TV cartoons with Roadrunner and Wile E. Coyote, I kinda expected a lot of sputtering and sparks, but the fuse burned inside and just smoked. We had ninety seconds to get back behind the truck. Dave started his stopwatch and blew the signal on his portable airhorn since a few spectators had gathered.

The crack of the first charge echoed back and forth through the narrow valley, followed almost instantly by the rest. For a moment the chimney stood still above all the commotion at its base. I glanced at Dave, wondering what went wrong. He wasn't even looking up but was eyeing the row of shacks. Then slowly the bricks began to crack with a hollow sound as the eighty-year-old mortar bonds began to separate and down she came. The shacks disappeared in an instant. What was once, now wasn't: their stories gone but safe from the vultures scratching around.

"Like I said. Homewrecker!" Dave grinned through the dust.

So what's the measure of a man like that? Playing with such high stakes each and every day, what does that leave him to give a woman? He didn't have a death wish. He drove sensibly, followed the WCB safety rules strictly, and kept his logbook up to date. Maybe playing with such stuff as nitro and gelignite made him more aware of his own mortality, how it could be snuffed by a small miscalculation. Maybe it made him live for the moment—and that moment now included me.

I had to know how far to push him, where his edges were, what set him off. For all I knew, he could be my last chance.

Driving back that night to the Four Pines Motel in Lillooet, Dave had his sunburnt arm out the window. The dusk air was heavy with sage coming in gentle over us. We had the radio on but it came and went with the bends in the road. Dave reached down and switched it off as if he wanted my full attention. He had it.

"I got a job offer up in the Yukon for the winter. Highway avalanche control. Sounds like fun."

Fun? Triggering off tons of ice and snow in semi-controlled chaos. Fun? The Yukon in the winter with all four hours of daylight and forty below. Some fun.

More gravel clattered under the truck. Maybe I should thank the moths. I still felt the fuzzy buggers crawling on me sometimes. I once saw a blown-up picture of the adult codling moth, all frilly antennae scanning for someone to ruin. If it hadn't been for them, though, I wouldn't be here now sitting in the comfortable silence with Dave. I conveniently forgot the thirty years in between, the two kids now adults and the stucco bungalow with the oaf.

Can you do that? Just put half your life away when it goes bad? Drop a brick chimney on it and erase your version in a cloud of flying debris? Mix up some kind of memory insecticide and spray it all gone?

Dave was talking again. "If you wanted to come, I could call you my apprentice and we'd make more money. One winter up there and we'd be rolling in the dough. Enough to do most anything you want."

So what did I want? No damn bugs and a good man to lie beside each and every night. Someone who doesn't get liquored up and nasty. Someone who asks me what I want.

Our last job of the summer was up in Prince George, at the pulp mill. Another stack to drop, but this one had to crumble straight down and it was big! We laid in the charges, connected the fuses and let 'er rip. When the dust settled, Dave looked worried.

"Shit, that was only seven. We loaded eight holes." How he could hear, let alone count, the individual explosions was beyond me, the apprentice.

Somewhere in the pile was a five-kilogram surprise for the excavator operator waiting to load out the shattered chunks and Dave couldn't let that happen. He told me to stay put while he took a look around.

He was about halfway across the shard-strewn field when it went off. He was sat down hard and cut with a bit of flyrock. By the time I reached him on a dead run, he was staggering to his feet and giving me that goofy grin, though a bit lopsided. The mill's first aid man was there with his kit and we fixed up the bleeding.

How do you give your heart to someone that might just evaporate? I didn't feel like starting over, making those first hesitant moves like we did at the Princeton Hotel for a few days late last spring, feeling all silly and shy. Going through that time of sneaking sideways sparrow looks at someone to size them up without appearing to.

Dave held onto my arm as we stumbled to the truck. I drove back to the motel on the hills south of town. We sat for a long time on the bed drinking a cold beer.

"That was a first. That misfire. Never had one before. Malfunction. Not our fault. There's some things you just can't predict or plan for." I squirmed around on the bed to face him. Things you can't foresee, forces beyond our control. Moths, defective fuses, errors in judgement, bad choices. How often do you get another chance?

With this warm man, the Yukon's not so cold. Forty-two below's killed the moths.

BUSES COME, BUSES GO

Near the end of the month, Ma started looking anxious. She walked through the house picking up a dish, looking at it as if considering its value and then setting it down. Running her fingers along the edge of the kitchen counter, she paused to stare out the back window to the yard where my younger brother, Tommy, stood in a wide-legged stance throwing a knife at the fence boards. The wood was more bruised than splintered, such was his skill, but he had little else to do.

"Faye," she said, turning back to where I was working on homework at the kitchen table. "If you were going on a magical voyage and could only take one suitcase of clothes, which ones would they be? Why don't we go and pack, just for fun."

But it wasn't ever fun. I knew what would follow.

We lived in a bland company house, identical to all the others in the neighbourhood. Pastel shades of tan, beige, taupe and grey. I wished for some shocking paint like the reserve houses down by the river, above the log booms. They were bright blue, red, even one pumpkin orange—just what was needed in this coastal town of dependable morning fog and afternoon rain. But the most vivid hues in our house were Ma's crimson nails, finger and toe, which she touched up every morning, mixing the pungent smell of polish with our breakfast of burnt toast. That, and the dusty whiff of face powder applied with her little soft brush. She was nearly the only woman in town so adorned. The rest of the dowdy housewives and working women stared when we shopped the day-olds at the Lucky Buck grocery store.

The town was just big enough to keep ahead of the absentee landlords and delinquent utility bills; this was our saving grace. The rollover of employees at the paper mill kept everyone in a constant coming and going. Ma never intended to skip out on rent. She'd say the colour of the paint gave her headaches, or there was a musty smell that could only come from rat droppings, or a neighbour's suspicious stare, or voices in the wall saying, "Go on. Git!"

Then we'd wait 'til after dark and scurry out to the car with a few suitcases. Ma slouched behind the wheel while Tommy and I pushed the car down the street before she'd start the engine and flip on the lights. "Just like the spies on TV," she'd giggle. Yeah, just like them.

But household budgeting was not one of her strengths. Maybe it was the bottle-blond hair permed into loose, billowy waves, or the rosebud lips she carefully coloured even on those mornings when there was absolutely nothing to call her out of the house. But whatever it was, she had the appearance of a perpetual little girl. Her looks, attitude and lack of merchantable skills belied her gritty ability to make do. She was not addled or simple, nothing that textbook. She just preferred her own reality to that offered her by circumstance. Mother of a daughter and a son, wife of a man who went north six years ago to work in the oil patch and never came back. He had been a general labourer at the mill but got laid off when the company changed hands, and they always started cutting jobs at the bottom. Occasionally, very occasionally, a money order arrived in a plain envelope. No letter, no return address and the smudged cancellation stamp gave no clues as to its origin. She'd smile, and wave it in front of me and Tommy as evidence that we were still a functioning unit. I knew better, but I still stared at his picture on the dresser and secretly hoped it could be true.

Ma stood for long periods looking out the front window at the steam rising from the mill stacks. Sometimes I pulled up a chair and joined her. The plume billowed out day and night, as hypnotic as the waves out on the west side of the Island; soothing too, as it never rolled out of the tall brick chimneys the same way. Depending on the wind, the heat of the day and the velocity of the vapour, it would be different colours, different textures—sometimes like a cauliflower head, other times, when the air was still, a spiral or layers like a sky sandwich. It never put up a fight against the wind. It couldn't, but worked with it to create fanciful clouds. I understood it.

The late-night packing and unpacking actually did help me, though. I learned what was needed and what was disposable, not only in underwear and tops, but the extraneous baggage of emotions. We listened to old records from the sixties—Simon & Garfunkel was a favourite. She knew all the words though she could not carry a tune in a bucket. I would hold a rolled-up movie magazine like a microphone and we'd lean our heads together and sing like the stars we watched on TV, before the repo man took it back.

The only embarrassing thing about all this midnight moving was having to go into the principal's office and report changes of address with such regularity. Mrs. Mc-Gimpsey, the secretary, looked up from the student information questionnaire after altering the street number once again.

"I guess I should use a pencil for your form, Faye. Easier to erase you then." I just smiled and nodded. I liked school a lot: the steamy jostling hallway, the implied glances of the cute boys and the elation when I got back an exam with a big red A at the top. I believed my teachers, who said education was the key to success—and success meant getting out of this mill town, with its distinctive smell of rotten eggs and cabbage, where the girls left school pregnant and their boyfriends entered the Dickensian paper factory to emerge forty years later, pasty faced and paunchy. I envisioned myself dressed in a crisp business suit making top-level decisions with people listening to my every word. And I was gorgeous, naturally, without a touch of mascara or lip gloss, just my copper-coloured curls. A genuine beauty.

There were days I dawdled after class, wanting to remain in the bright classrooms and the science labs with their exotic chemical sharpness. At home, especially in the long, drab winters, we often had to unscrew a light bulb from the socket in one room and take it while stumbling in the dark to the next because Ma couldn't afford to buy more. Not that there was ever much to trip over. Unless the apartment or house was furnished, we had to improvise with crates and boxes. But I never felt despair. Ma loved Tommy and me and provided the best she could. It was not her fault Daddy left us, though in the occasional adolescent screaming fit, I threw that into her perfectly made-up face.

She and Tommy never fought. He was quiet and often got bullied at school, which surprised me since he was big and strong like Daddy. He sometimes confided in me that as soon as he was able, he was quitting school to head north to work. And to look for his tall, good-looking, red-haired papa, I knew.

Before the TV was repossessed, Ma sat and watched it for hours, no matter what was on—news, weather, soap operas or talk shows. Oprah reruns came on mid-afternoon, and often when I came home, I'd find her sobbing into a tea towel.

"Oh, Faye. This poor lady on the show. Her husband ran off with another woman—her best friend—leaving her with four kids and one is taken up with polio and the others are running wild. She only needs two hundred bucks for medicine and I'm going to send her some. Poor thing. Come here, my darling, let me hold you. I know we don't have much, but we are healthy and together."

Yeah, I thought, together and wearing clothes too old to be fashionable, too new to be retro and we're real healthy eating No Name brand KD for a week. Quick, easy and cheap.

During the summer, the valley switched its weather from cold and wet to hot and dry. The forests crisped up quickly and filled the town with shut-down loggers, frustrated and drunk. Hanging out on the hard plastic benches outside the bus station was a favourite summer activity for me and my best friend, Agnes, whose house is bright red. Funny how so many of the kids down there have such outdated names. Makes them seem older than they are, but sometimes what's in those brown eyes does too.

We'd play this game as we sipped our canned pop. When the bus pulled in from across the Hump, we'd invent stories for the people getting off or on.

"This guy in the rumpled suit. He's in trouble in Vancouver. He was a hotshot car salesman but was embezzling money from the company. See how he looks around so quickly? Definitely on the run. He thought he was safe even though the boss knew about it, 'cause he knew the boss was having an affair with the secretary, but eventually the boss's marriage failed and the boss didn't care about who knew what and came after him for the missing money. Which is in that briefcase he's holding so tight."

When the passengers queued up to board the departing bus, we'd giggle behind our hands and wonder who was leaving and why. It was still a small enough town that we usually knew at least one person, coming or going.

"That's the substitute teacher from the reserve school. She was nice. But some of the boys were a bit hard on her. She didn't try to let them do much, though. Kept with the program. Good. But now she's leaving. Maybe back to the city or a patient boyfriend. But when she gets there, he has another lover. Just before she is gonna jump off the Lions Gate Bridge, he realizes she is the one for him and they make up, right there above the First Narrows."

The best time was late evening after the last bus ground its gears up the hill toward the darkening mountain pass. The metal sign over the station clicked and snapped as it cooled down. Bugs swarmed around the bare bulbs. Out of the six, only four worked, the others smashed and useless. There was always something exciting happening at the nearby bars—drunks being kicked out, women yelling at their dates. One night, like a roiling boil of insects, a pack of men, yelling and shoving, stumbled out of the Kingsway Hotel pub. We watched them for a moment, but like most drunken brawls, this was more bluster than blood.

Heading home late at night, after all the excitement, we would talk about where we would travel, if we could go anywhere we wanted, what we'd do if we had all the money in the world. The practicalities of our dreams.

Eventually Agnes and I won scholarships to UBC and made ready to leave. Ma and Tommy came down to the bus station to see me off. Ma's eyes were all red and smudged from crying and laughing. Tommy just shoved his hands in the pockets of his oversized hip-hop pants and stared at the sidewalk. The incoming bus hissed to a stop on the other side of the building and I stooped to pick up my two suitcases—all I could really call my own.

"Faye, here, take this. I've decided I don't need it no more." She shoved a small cosmetic mirror set at me. "I know you don't use makeup, but every now and then a lady has to look her best. To take advantage of any opportunities."

I smiled, opening and closing it with a satisfying snap. "Thanks, Ma. I'll write when I get to Vancouver and settled." A call would be quicker but our phone was long since disconnected. Ma was on a list.

The line of incoming passengers was walking away from us and without thinking, I started cooking up scenarios for them. The two old folks helping each other walk as they had for sixty years, the teenagers with shopping bags half full of shoplifted booty from the east side mall, and the shuffling, hunched-over man in a turned-up hoody with one sleeve pinned in half, like old Mr. Erickson with the

Legion in the Canada Day parade. Lost his arm in Korea, he once said. I knew what he meant, but always wondered how you could lose a part of your body, like you'd lose a book or sweater. Like how people would say, "Oh, sadly, The Drink took him." Who or what was it that took him, and where did they go?

I boarded the bus, found a window seat and waited with my eyes closed until the rumble increased and we eased out of the parking lot heading to my new life. I thumbed open the small mirror and in its circle I saw Ma and Tommy watching the bus leave. I turned the mirror slightly and saw the arrivals mixing with the leave-takers. The man with the pinned sleeve limped toward Ma and Tommy and flipped back his hood with the one good arm. Ma's lips made a big O.

I'd know his red hair anywhere.

I closed the little round mirror with a crisp snap.

UNCLIPPED

Brian hobbled up to the double doors of the Eldorado Hotel and paused before pulling on the brass handles. A cane supported him on a good day, crutches on a bad.

Here we go again, he thought, same old gang, and same old questions. This must be what it was like when Mel was pregnant with the kids, even total strangers acting like her belly was communal property, asking dumb, personal questions. Now it's my turn to be on display. Like having a public affliction, this stooped posture, this limping shuffle now mine. Always the irritating questions, always the need to share their own experience. Like I fucking care.

Company New Year's Eve party, Mel home with the kids. Some fun. Just wash down the Tylenol 3s with Lucky Lager and try to make a go of it. I suppose Ali will be here, with her words of condolence and sorrow. For me or for her own sake? Crocodile tears hiding the accusation of screwing up her perfect safety record. I wish she'd let it go. Wasn't really her fault. Or mine. Or anyone's. Shit happens.

Three months ago, he was working on a new water tank for the town. Scaffolding weaved around the structure and a crane lifted pieces up to the crew. Cutthroat times in the construction industry, with companies low-ball bidding just to keep their workers from fleeing to Fort Mac and the big bucks. Profit margins sliced like the thin bologna in his lunchbox sandwiches. Not that he even had time to stop and eat. Grab a bite on the run, slam back a swig of coffee from his battered Thermos, keep moving, keep production on schedule.

From the top of the tower, Brian stole a moment to look at the view. To the east was the blue of the Strait backdropped by the mainland mountains with their dusting of early snow. He eagerly anticipated winter shutdown, when he would put one toddler in the backpack and the other on the wooden toboggan and snowshoe the local hills. Closer to the tower was a wall of trees, the firs green and unchanging through the swing of seasons, the alders and cottonwoods already bare-limbed. Two eagles perched below him and he grinned from his unusual position of high advantage. He liked these private amusements, personal moments within himself. Reserved by nature, when he and Mel married, it was a stretch to open up even to his newly beloved.

Frost coated the catwalk and scaffold planks with a crusty rime. He walked carefully around the edge of the tower, wearing his bulky tool belt of wrenches and bolts to assemble the dome segments slowly rising on a cable guided by his hand signals: thumb right or left, a pinching motion to go slow, circles in the air with his index finger up for lifting, down for lowering. Logical manoeuvres. He kept his eyes on the steel panel, slowly swinging as it approached, and glanced down now and then to make eye contact with the crane operator and give him a nod.

He wore his regulation body harness, clipped into the steel security rail. He hated the cumbersome strapping that often tangled in his legs. But Alison, the first aid and safety geek with her white hardhat, showed up at the oddest times and if he was unclipped it was shit creek—docked wages, and if it happened again, termination. Then it was north to the pipelines, four weeks in, one week out. Alison and her checklist: got your steel-toed boots, high-viz vest, new six-point suspension hardhat with chinstrap and, always, the harness? Alison and her clipboard full of WorkSafe forms and her clean coveralls.

As the morning warmed, the breeze picked up. If it got too strong, they'd have to shut down and find other parts of the job to do. But getting the dome covered was a priority and he and the others hustled to bolt it together.

One of those moments, bewildering in its complexity: a gust of wind caught the panel. Suddenly four tons of steel swung at him, scraping along the rail, sparks coming off the pipe like a welding torch. The railing buckled and broke and his safety clip slid toward the gap at the same time the panel hit his shoulder, pushing him over the edge. Stunned by the impact, he watched dumbly as the clip came off and he was in the air.

He had heard the stories about how your life flashes before your eyes, how the film replays the regrets and joys of experience, but little of that happened to Brian. He flailed through the air, clawing at the riveted side of the tank as he plummeted. He was thinking of the landing, and the piles of bedding sand around the tank. Sand. He remembered for an instant the beaches of the Baja where he and Mel went on their honeymoon, the soft, white, warm sand where they lazed, watching the whales and their new calves breaching in the tepid lagoon. Soft sand.

When he hit there were no whales, no drinks with swizzle sticks, and no lovely, tanned Mel smelling of coconut oil. White-hot light, unbelievable impact and sounds throughout his whole body. His tool belt gouged divots in his waist. He heard muffled yelling. No pain. Not yet. He lay flat on his back, struggling to breathe, eyes squinted shut and tears gushing out. Fuck, fuck, fuck. Hot, then cold rushes.

"Don't move, buddy. Stay still," someone shouted. "First Aid's coming."

But he had to move, had to see how bad it was. Fists uncurled, and then tightened up. Toes in his workboots wiggled. His feet rolled from one side to the other. Good so far. His head leaned left, then right. No crunching or crackling. Then came the black rush of staggering pain, legs going tingly and fuzzy. His hurried lunch boiled up sour in his throat. He woke staring at the hospital lights in the surgical recovery room.

A week in post-op then rehab with everyone telling him how lucky he was. *Just* four broken ribs, a couple ruptured discs, and a few displaced vertebrae pinned, bolted and patched together. *Just*. And then came the grinding pain every minute, every second. They promised it would diminish with time and pills. Not bad for a three-storey dive, they said. *How lucky*.

Alison said she had to talk to him, but he didn't want to see her, did not want to face the regulations, the questions, the implied carelessness. Now the New Year's party, three months later—the first time he had to see the crew, the crane operator, the boss, anyone else from the job site.

After rehab, he had gone on short walks around their neighbourhood, avoiding dogs and people. Always the same stupid comments about recovery strategies.

"You should try yoga, yogurt, yarrow leaves. You should do tai chi. Qigong. Acupuncture, acupressure." Everyone's a fucking expert. Everyone has a story. You should. You should. Amazing the English language has such a useless word as "should" and such wonderful ones like "chocolate" and "coffee."

"You're limping."

"What's with the cane?"

"Got a bad back? My uncle/father/cousin has/had a..."

Everyone wants you to stand there and patiently listen to their story as the barbed wire tightens around the new metal in your spine, as the red-hot poker runs from your squinting eyes to your toes. When standing and listening are the worst things imaginable. Fill in the words while he stands there throbbing and gritting his teeth. Pain erasing tact.

On those nights when he could not sleep, when the pills did a cranial rodeo, he'd think up responses designed to stun and silence. Then he'd wake up sweating and frustrated. Now the goddamned party. More interrogations, as if he had no other components of a life but a shattered spine. Nothing else going on. Always the first words: "How's the back? How's the goddamned back?" Just great, fuckoff; I'm more than that. I'm still Brian and he is tired, so very tired of being seen only as a casualty.

When people ask "How are you?" they aren't really concerned with you. They want a simple "Fine." Or "Oh, not bad." So they can swing the conversation back around to their own situation.

He pushed open the doors and walked through the lobby toward the ballroom, although words like "lobby" and "ballroom" were too grand for this place. The chairs around the registration desk were worn and mismatched, the magazines on the coffee table months old, and several light bulbs were burnt out. Tinny music echoed from the party room as he shuffled in. Knots of people gathered in the corners and hunched over tables, ignoring the No Smoking signs, using empty beer cans for ashtrays.

    He didn't know how to behave. Aching made him crazy. Seemed like just yesterday he was driving his pickup again for the first time, and he gapped out at a green traffic light, still riding the painkillers' sweet caress. The driver behind him laid on the horn and flipped him the finger. Brian glanced into the rear-view mirror, slipped the truck into reverse and popped the clutch, driving his ten-gauge steel trailer hitch and the round chrome ball through the front grille of the impatient car. Sat there for a moment listening to the car's fan destroying itself on the crumpled radiator. The driver sat open-mouthed and not moving. Brian waited a polite moment then drove off. Two blocks later a police car with flashing lights pulled him over.

    "Didja just do what that guy told me?"

    "Is this really about that or is it just because you got a short dick and try to make up for it by wearing a badge and a gun?"

    Mel came down and bailed him out, explained the fall, injury and rehab, and they let him off with a suspension and a court order for twenty hours of community service. (Mel didn't mention the codeine.)

    "So where do I do this service?"

    "Go down to St. Ignatius Church. Iggy's. Ask to see Molly."

    "When do I start?"

"Soon as your doctor gives you the go-ahead. Let us know."

Next day, Brian drove to the church and saw the crowd waiting. Some children among the adults. A tall woman greeted them as they entered; some with a handshake, others a gentle hug or a wide smile.

Brian hobbled up the concrete steps, looking carefully at his feet. He explained his court order, expecting some sort of disapproval or judgement but receiving none.

"Welcome, Brian. I had a phone call mentioning your need for light-duty jobs. We'll start you off as an Open Hand, a greeter of our daily clients. Table and chair waiting for you just inside the door. Your job will be to inform them of all the services we offer besides hot soup. No sign-up sheet, no proof of identity, no charges, only a pleasant visit with people who may've spent the night in a cardboard box under the bridge. Washrooms are over there. I'll be around if you need any help."

He read the newsletter listing everything Iggy's provided: breakfast for school kids, soup and sandwiches for others, counselling, health referrals, legal aid, employment opportunities.

Sitting at this table talking to the men and women was more tiring than his construction job. Yet the hours flew past and the painkillers wore off unnoticed. Some of the hard-living stories astounded him, others he decided were well-practised bullshit, used for street survival. He rose from the chair, groaning with the return of the hot steel in his back and hips.

Molly met him as he was leaving.

"Long day for the first time. Know you've made several

people happier just listening to them. See you again when you are rested. It takes more than muscle strength to do this mission."

He nodded and again carefully navigated the steps to Mel, waiting in their truck. It was an early autumn afternoon and the air had a cool edge to it, but Mel had found a swath of sunshine and sat comfortably. Their two children, strapped in their car seats, squealed when Daddy appeared with his crutches—his stilts, they called them.

"Well, how did it go? Longer than I thought you'd be there."

Brian nodded and chewed up his pills. After a few minutes of silence, he told her about the hurt and lame, the dispossessed, the invisible ones who took his hurt as their own.

"You look… more at ease, somehow. That's different, anyway."

"Brian, over here," yelled one of his old crew. He hobbled over to the table, his right leg being dragged by the momentum of his torso. "Buy you a beer, buddy. Good to see you out and about."

"Yeah, words fail me." He immediately regretted the sarcasm. These guys had nothing to do with the fall. No one did and that was the bitch of the situation, no one to hang it on. Even the crane operator couldn't have seen the invisible gust. That'd make it easier, Brian thought, if there was someone to thump, someone to say, "You sonovabitch." But no. Just the rehab techs saying how good he was doing, just the doc saying how lucky he was, just Mel trying to take care of two toddlers and him, her compassion and patience wearing thin. Going from still to shrill in an instant.

In the dictionary, "sympathy" lies between "suppository" and "syphilis."

That was it. Everything that happened was so fucking understandable. It all made perfect logic to everyone but him.

"Yeah, beer. Make it a couple cold ones."

They went down smooth, as did the next four. Things began to make more sense. He had a question and he lurched to his unsteady feet. Fuck the crutches.

"Where is she?"

"Who?"

"Alison, said she wanted to talk to me, said it was important. But y'see, I've been kinda busy. Might say unavailable. I got... issues."

"Easy, Brian. She took it real hard... you were the first bad accident she ever had. Worse than when Alfie lost his thumb in the cut-off saw."

"Hard? The landing was hard, Thanksgiving in rehab was hard, feeling hardware in my bones is hard. Then Christmas." No going out in the bush with the family to find the perfect tree. The scent of needles and sap. Only lying on the couch giving grumpy directions on hanging the ornaments—egg carton angels, painted macaroni designs with flaking glitter. "Watching it all pass by. That was hard. Missing out on lives. Hard."

"Ali has it all, too. Hard, that is. Cuts close to home for her too. The drunk driver killing her brother on his bike. Him lying in the ditch for an hour. That's what made her become a First Aid."

"Well—" Brian didn't know what to say to that. "What does she want to talk to me about?"

"Guess you gotta ask her. She's right behind you."

Brian didn't hear Ali walk up because of the deejay's music and hired chatter. He turned to face the woman, his anger looking to paint a bull's eye on her if she said one word, one word of accusation, anything to even hint of blame.

"Brian..."

"Ali..."

They stood staring at each other; she began to cry. Half of him wanted to put his tattooed arms around her, half of him tried to compose the cruellest thing he could possibly say—but nothing came out.

"How's the kids?" she asked finally. "Mel?"

A life, getting my life back. My life. My back. I am still me.

INTO THE SILVERTHRONE CALDERA

I have been witness to things great and beyond understanding or reason. But nothing prepared me for this. For her.

That summer I got a job as a log grader and second loader in the drop zone of a heli-logging show up-coast at Knight Inlet. The Klinaklini River valley at the head of the inlet is a place of superlatives: majestic, glacier-capped Mount Waddington rearing up four thousand metres from riverside thickets, grizzly bears the size of cars with little fear of puny, scampering men, trees like the pillars of Solomon's temple, felled and waiting for our arrogant, noisy machines in the air and on the ground, and men with big stories, as if we were masters of these great things.

Though surrounded by such grandeur and taken in by our confidence, we often suspected a dreadful power lurked beneath, behind or beside our work. Some problems were mechanical, logistical or pure folly, but the rest remained in the mystery of place.

But we hardly ever talked about it for fear of appearing weak.

Every night was the same. The deep fjord lost its heat quicker than the valley, drawing the warm interior air in gusts through the flailing riverside cottonwoods, in past the wet, black noses of the sleek cinnamon bears sifting it for messages of opportunity or threat, blasting in to test our resolve. It blew without ceasing, as if it took our presence personally. It slammed into the camp scow like a clenched fist, letting up only when it paused to gain strength or change direction. Then, even the bowed trees seemed surprised and stood confused but relieved.

Lying in our narrow beds in the bunkhouse, we listened to the outflow wind pushing fiercely against the creaking and groaning hull, straining the cables like fiddle strings singing taut. Knowing if the rusty wires ever snapped, our whole camp—bunkhouse, cook shack and supply sheds—would be driven down the inlet and capsized by the gale-driven waves.

An exhalation more like a howl, a wail. Every night was the same.

Then came the magic hour. The land air was equally exhausted. The wind had emptied itself. Spent. Although the sun was still hidden behind the eastern ramparts, the sky brightened. Daylight flowed down like golden syrup, waking some animals and signalling others to seek refuge. It shimmered through the treetops, making prismed light off the droplets of sap and night dew. But when it reached the fallen monarchs, it lost its luminescence and became flat and listless.

After too short a night, the bell sounded and, fuzzy-headed and bleary-eyed, we stumbled in our slippers to the cookhouse to lard up for the day facing us.

"She was a howler last night, eh?" one of the pilots remarked as we waited in line like obedient beasts. "Hope she doesn't build up like that today, but she probably will." She. The presence of a looming matriarch calling the shots.

He was one of the American crew the company had imported with their aircraft to harvest this valuable block before the bugs got into it. We had become friends through casual conversation, sensing common interests beyond logs, favourite brands of beer and inflated sexual conquests. Not just a "camp friend" made out of desperation, the sort you'd cross the street in town to avoid.

We shovelled the breakfast load into still-sleeping stomachs then filed into the lunchroom, where more tables of food awaited. Made sandwiches, grabbed yesterday's greasy, cold pork chops and chicken, a half-dozen oranges and apples, cookies, slices of pie and cake soon to be crushed to a sticky pulp. Filled a couple of Thermoses with tea or coffee, stuffed it all into a knapsack with some dry clothes and rain gear, and returned to the bunkhouse to gear up. I glanced longingly at the bed that would not be mine for another twelve to fourteen hours. Then on with the caulk boots and safety pants, grabbed my hardhat to join the crew boarding the crummy for the bouncing ride over potholes and washboard up to the landing—where the voracious worst of the insect world waited.

Never needed a timepiece. Like union brothers, these flying butchers have regular shifts you could set a watch by: blackflies and no-see-ums start the day, then as the breeze picks up, they hand the torment to the slightly more robust mosquitoes. With rising temperatures comes the main assault—big horseflies and deltoid-winged deerflies who are not content to merely sting or suck blood. They want chunks of my salty flesh. Hovering around until I am in a position of vulnerability then biting down through my shirt where my suspenders cross and rub. When stunned with a fast slap, they suffer creative, but dark, vengeance. Kill one, the swarm reinforces.

We were logging a steep hillside of first-growth fir, cedar and hemlock that had been beyond the reach of earlier generations of hungry loggers, their wooden spar trees and steam-pot donkey engines spooling in logs as far as the cable reached. Now, with the heavy-lift heli, nothing was inaccessible. Nothing was sacred, we bragged. It had been felled a year before so the logs could dry out for the monstrous, dragonfly-shaped Sikorsky S-64 Skycrane. Besides this aerial workhorse were two smaller helis, a Bell 206 Jet Ranger and a Hughes 500. They sat waiting like well-trained but anxious hounds. Even their drooping rotor tips reminded me of the ears on my sad yellow Lab each time my wife drove me to the seaplane dock to fly out for another shift.

Our caravan of crew buses, mechanical trucks, fuel tankers and clanking log trucks bumped up to the drop zone and service landing. We got out and stared at the sky in hopes it would remain clear and calm, but maybe deep in our hearts, our tired hearts, we hoped the fog would roll in as it often did, or the inflow wind would exceed the limits for flying.

Many a day started out as hopeful. We'd arrive at the landings, watch the bears watching us while the aircrew ran their checks and serviced the helis. Maybe we'd get one or two loads off but then I'd feel a dampness on my neck. A moist hand lying lightly. I'd turn to look down the valley cleft toward the fjord to see a blue-grey wall of oily and cold marine fog quickly rolling up toward us, as if beckoned by a promise from the warm valley's cleavage, unaware that like the temptations of a fickle lover, the bid to embrace would later be reversed. But for us, the day would be a write-off anyway.

"Seems like something is watching us, just waiting until we get the birds running, the men up the slope, everyone in place then fucking fog or fucking wind," lamented the management to no one, to everyone. As if it was our fault.

He'd hurriedly radio the helis, shouting at them to get down before the murk covered us. Sometimes they did, sometimes she was too fast and solid for mere vapour and we heard them rattling around above us, looking for a hole before they ran out of fuel. If no opening was quickly found, they'd get chased up the valley by the pursuing fog, land on the road, and wait like broody vultures. It might burn off in a half hour or squat over us for the day. But the clock kept running, the dollars bleeding away. Headache, our manager, would run around hassling everyone from the cook to us guys on the landing, but steering clear of the indispensable aircrew. We peons were just expendable grist. The chokermen on the sidehill perched in the slash, waiting for Headache's decision, then walked down through a steep kilometre of shattered forest. Swearing all the way.

Downtime was both welcome and cursed. When she clamped a thick lid on the Klinaklini or when her daytime inhale was as fierce as the nocturnal snores, we stayed grounded. Physically, morally, financially. No work, no logs. No logs, no pay. What to do? Back to camp. Slip off the hot boots and play pool on the worn table with four balls missing, try to get the satellite dish re-aimed after last night's battering, go back to our cells and thumb through magazines. Clip yellowed toenails. Pace.

Pilot and I searched for reading material in lunchroom boxes. He found a picture book of local geological phenomena.

"Look at this!"

There was a two-page spread of a harsh and pitiless landscape, a rocky, ice-covered bowl rimmed by fanged palisades. It gave me the shivers just looking at it.

"Northwest of Knight Inlet, in the Garibaldi Volcano Belt, is the Silverthrone Caldera," I read in the caption. "A collapsed dome of a dormant, but potentially active, volcano crusted by a fragile layer of brittle cooled magma. It covers hundreds of square kilometres. If the caldera is still venting fumes and deep magma, a slight precipitating event could produce an eruption of catastrophic dimensions."

"Now that would be cool to see," Pilot said. He gave me a little suggestive grin. "Silver throne. Maybe that's where she lives, the feral goddess of the valley."

"Yeah, but what would be an event that would set her off?"

"Rotor downwash? Drop a big cedar log on her?"

I continued to read the next paragraph. "Steam eruptions and poisonous gases are released through fumaroles by a series of minor earthquakes and shifting volcanic debris. Boiling water streams emerge throughout the caldera.

"Here the possibility of violent, unpredictable change is the only constant."

Nice neighbours, I thought, but didn't say.

Mountain flying is not for the inexperienced or foolish. Downdrafts, katabatic gales, wind shears to be dealt with.

I once asked Pilot where he learned to fly helis. "Nam," he replied, but little more. Later, when we were linked by helmet earphones and mics, he said the only guys who talked a lot about that jungle war were either not there or had sat at a desk growing hemorrhoids in some big base like Da Nang and were evac'd before the whole fucking fiasco collapsed in '75. So, yanking old-growth fir off a mountainside seemed less risky than Viet Cong rockets and shellfire, but he still wore the ace of spades on his helmet.

Today, when there was the slightest light in the east, the helis fired up their turbines, thirty-metre rotors churning up a maelstrom of dust, wood chunks and debris. First, the smaller Jet Ranger lifted off, taking the chokermen up the mountainside with a sling of cables under the chopper. Those guys were mountain goats, scrambling over the tangle of felled trees to lasso logs before the big hook slung under the Sikorsky arrived. Once in the air, it snatched a bundle of full tree-length logs off the mountainside. The loadmaster in his rear-facing bubble called out the weights on the longline—seven thousand, ten, twelve grand—and the dragonfly dove for the landing, five big blades chomping at the air.

A push of a button on the control stick dropped the logs like giant pick-up sticks in the drop zone where a front-end loader quickly gathered them and spread them out on a set of skid logs. We frantically cut them into preferred lengths. Another loader cleared the skids and hustled them to an oversized off-highway logging truck. I ran across the landing to throw on the cable straps, made a quick notation in my tally book and hurried back to the skids as the next load was spread and the heli was augering back up the mountain for another. It is an expensive way to log, so the target was to process a load cycle every three to five minutes, pausing only when the bird stopped for refuelling and we did too. Gulp a sandwich, inhale a swallow of tea or water. Same tango, every day, follow the plan.

On this particular day, we did. Then all hell broke loose.

The S-64 carries fuel in neoprene bags in its spraddled legs. More fuel means less lift for the logs, weight being crucial. So, they only fill up with enough Jet A for an hour's cycle. The fuelling and service landing was adjacent to the drop zone. There was the fuel tanker, the shop truck with parts and tools for the birds, a storage van and several pickups for the ground and flight crews. When the Sikorsky comes in for fuel, the crew (pilot, co-pilot and loadmaster) leaves the heli for safety reasons. But rather than shut down the huge turbines and wait for the blades to stop spinning (time is money), they friction-lock them into a no-lift flat pitch and climb down. The Kenworth tanker with thousands of litres of Jet A drives up and delivers the juice.

But for some reason, on this day, while the fuel was gurgling into the tanks, the blades slipped into gear and the bird started to lift. With no one at the controls, it took a couple of sideways crow hops, the portside leg crumpled and the blades sliced into the tanker, igniting the fuel instantly. Five hundred metres away with my back to the disaster, I felt the tremendous *whoomph* and turned to see a column of smoke and fire instantly churning into the clear blue sky. Both the Sikorsky and the tanker were fully engulfed.

The heli is built with high-tech materials—magnesium, aluminum, titanium and alloys—all of which burn white-hot. As the fire crept into the turbine, the still-rotating gearbox and spinning rotor hub started to come apart. With tremendous screeching and squalling, cogs, shafts, pieces of housing and rotors whirred off in all directions as we stood gaping at the firestorm. A garbage-can-sized piece of shrapnel had blown through the shop truck, scattering tools and parts all over the landing. Jet A from the tanker was pouring out into the gravel of the landing and popping up all around, then it would ignite, spouting geysers of flame.

Nearby was an old snub-nosed Chev tanker full of the more flammable gasoline for the pickups. The flames were creeping closer when one of the crew hopped in and tried to start it but, as misfortune often gathers more calamities, it had a dead battery. The ferociously burning Kenworth at least was sliced open, but the gas truck was fully loaded and battened down—a huge bomb waiting to go off.

A loader operator saw the situation, raced his machine to the inferno, drove the log forks through the front of the Chev, and reversed it to safety. By now the rest of us had stopped staring, dumbfounded, and began throwing firefighting equipment into a truck. But facing the flames with a little Wajax Mark 4 pump and a puny hose seemed a futile effort. Watching nervously for those little pop-ups of fire in the gravel around us, we just hosed down the perimeter and hoped it would burn itself out.

Perhaps the she-god of that rugged country took pity on us, for that was the only afternoon all season when there was no rising wind up the valley, which would have spread the blaze into the surrounding mountainside of tinder-dry felled and bucked logs to create a firestorm of unquenchable proportion. Eventually the immense Forest

Service Martin Mars water bomber thundered overhead, warning siren blaring, and we vacated the area. Two drops and the fire was quenched. All that remained was a section of tail rotor, one wheel strut with a tire, and various parts strewn about. I don't know if they ever found any trace of the Kenworth driver—a big, jovial guy who had no chance to run.

That afternoon, Pilot and I walked around the smouldering wreckage, saying nothing, avoiding the others. We knew the show was over. We were to be sent home by plane and boat the next morning as the investigators and coroner flew in.

Pilot kept muttering: "It's not possible. He wouldn't forget the lock. He's a pro. Done this hundreds of times. There's the shutdown checklist. And the co-pilot doubling up everything. Someone must've undone the clamp. Why?"

"Someone? Something?" I asked. He turned to stare at me.

He looked at the parked Jet Ranger and then over the valley toward the wall of peaks.

"Take a scenic tour? Last chance. Cumulus clouds building up, though. Could be a bit bumpy."

I nodded and within minutes we were lifting off at the machine's max rate of climb. Below lay the riverside grassland criss-crossed by ancient grizzly trails. Generations of paws in the exact same prints. Our clear-cut pocked the landscape like mange. Looking through the bubble I saw men scurrying around the crash site, picking up remnants and salvage. The orange helmets and safety vests of the chokermen struggled toward the landing. Like bugs. Our swarm. Swatted.

We lifted until the timber thinned out and alpine avalanche chutes cut lines down the steepening slopes. Then no trees, just sparse grass patches on flat ledges. Then just rock and ice. A bothersome horsefly buzzed against the glass. Out of habit I squashed him dead.

We eventually crested the ridge and there lay the Silverthrone Caldera below us. Suddenly the heli gave a convulsive, stomach-churning lurch as we dipped the nose into the bowl. More solid than a thermal speed bump. A direct slap.

Pilot flailed the controls around as the heli wobbled and mushed from one side to another. The altimeter was unwinding rapidly. I heard his fast breathing in my earphone. My own heart beat faster.

"Going down. Hold on," Pilot yelled.

Desperately we both scanned the rocky caldera for a level spot but only saw broken talus and aprons of scree weathered by wind and frost heave. Ground proximity alarm bleating. Fifty metres of thin alpine air above the flinty rock, so close we smelled the sulfur and brimstone, then the impotent rotors caught something solid and we rocketed up like a cartoon elevator. My ears popped. All the instruments going crazy but we were climbing. Not dropping into the maw of Silverthrone. Rotor torque in the red zone. Climbing faster than the Allison turbo was capable.

Someone. Something.

The black shroud of the crash was jarred loose, and the dizzy kick of being so close to annihilation twice in one day, of good fortune, of still being among the warm and breathing, flooded me with raw adrenalin.

"Maybe she was just saying hello," Pilot stammered.

"Or goodbye."

"Or fuck off and don't come back. I think I pissed myself."

Clearing the rimrock, we swooped back down toward the wagging finger of titanium smoke.

DELTA CHARLIE

On my fire warden patrol route for the Forest Service, I stop to check the Wolf Lake campground. At most of these guerrilla sites on my route, you will not find much in the way of Gore-Tex, Tilley hats or Mountain Equipment Co-op miracle fabric outerwear. Nor will you find expensive lightweight tents with high-tech rain flys sheltering portable espresso makers for the morning latte, organic soy milk, no sweetener. The summer citizens of Wolf, Blue Grouse and Hairtrigger Lakes do not wear sensible hiking boots. They do not carry adjustable trekking poles. Kraft Dinner and Costco bulk wieners are eaten more by necessity than choice. Gourmet freeze-dried linguine and sparkling chardonnay are absent from the daily menu.

They are well tattooed. The body art is not tiny or subtle, nor is it a Sanskrit mantra, an astrological symbol or a Celtic knot design. It says "Chantal Forever" or "Born to Party" and includes at least one grinning skull with encircling barbed wire. Barely controlled cellulite spews over Harley-Davidson belt buckles and strains bikinis. Their tenuous shelters are held together by duct tape and twine. You will not find them in a drum circle at a healing retreat, and if they walk in circles it is due to Lucky Lager more than a blissed-out meditative shuffle through a sacred labyrinth.

They drive sagging rust-bucket vehicles with bad tires and I marvel at how they ever insinuated them over the corduroy washboard and baby-headed logging roads to these lakes.

It is full summer and they have taken flight from the three-storey walk-up apartments in town with the tiny lobbies, broken gaping mailboxes, peeling lino and stained walls. Where idle men in undershirts and mullets slouch over iron railings, eighties rock anthems blare from open doors with holes punched through, faded photocopies of eviction notices lie crumpled on thresholds. This lakeside squat is their affordable escape. The water is clean and the air doesn't stink of rental mould and fried bologna.

The family structure may be ill-defined—moms with new boyfriends, dads with visitation rights—but these people are having a good time. Often they are the ones with rakes and shovels picking up garbage and returnable bottles left by weekend revellers marinated in the deadly mixture of testosterone, alcohol and gasoline. A sweet little girl helps clean up the residue from an abandoned camper torched on the weekend; a young boy in a dirty T-shirt is thrilled with the Smokey pins and decals I hand out.

My Forest Service boss in Campbell River estimates there are at least a hundred people living more or less permanently around the district's lakes and bush roads. Some are skipping out on rent, on spouses, on the tiresome details of survival—and occasionally on life itself. Existence becomes subsistence, and the last stand is often an old motorhome with payments long past due. They find an overgrown road down to a pothole lake, somehow wiggle the Wilderness Explorer into place and, like an exhausted kneeling camel, there it stays, sprouting plywood and blue tarp add-ons. Cheap tin stoves and free firewood fight the creeping coastal dampness and perhaps the despair. Visiting hours are not available, but suspicious glares are free.

I have found myself in remote road dead ends where a clandestine chop shop is set up to switch engines with ground-off serial numbers not matching the crudely repainted Camaros and BMWs. Oil, antifreeze and transmission fluid stain the gravel and seep into the lakes that are the drinking water for downstream towns. Other shacks and old buses house the twitchy, often armed, gardeners of the outdoor grow shows producing BC's most lucrative agricultural crop.

For my own safety I thumb the truck radio. "Patrol One, this is Quinsam Five at Little Goose Lake. Delta Charlie." In the phonetic jargon of the airways, this stands for the letters D and C. Dubious Characters. A bit of a slur, but the women on the base radio, the guardian angels in the white trailer beneath the big aerial, know what I mean and listen attentively for my next check-in.

It would be easy but erroneous to denigrate these people as low-class or less deserving of my regard and protection. It would be like yelling at the clouds that bring the lightning. Yes, these are my clients: mine for safekeeping as much as the mountainside fir and cedar, the elegant elk and cutthroat trout.

They live on abandoned road allowances, bush camps and common lands throughout the province—victims of a collapsing primary economy poorly replaced by McJobs and seasonal service or retail work not even covering the court orders. They sell off the motorbikes and speedboats bought while riding the gravy train, then mortgage the house for half its value, hoping the train will somehow loop around and let them swing back on board, but it never does. Eventually the wives get tired of the husbands going crazy with drink and desperation, and they split with the kids for the parents if they'll take them in, and to the shelter if they won't. Not that Ma and Pa are any wiser; they just grew up in a time when life offered better chances.

Theirs is a stretch of forsaken highway severed from the flow of vehicles by concrete barriers, like an oxbow lake formed in the elbow of a meandering mountain river. Cut off, but accessible if you look for the signs—tire tracks squeezing between the scruffy ditch line poplar and shimmering willow, the glimpse of tarnished chrome through the trees.

Once through the brush, I drive slowly past several decrepit Winnebagos, trailers with flat tires and expired licence plates, stained campers on corroded trucks with sagging springs. A face appears silhouetted in a grimy window then ducks back. Languid dogs watch from the ends of frayed ropes tied to rusty bumpers. The sky is a flat, dirty white, casting no shadows, no definition of light or dark, blurring social edges. It is like post-Chernobyl—these once-proud rolling palaces now soot-streaked, road-weary and furtive. One couple lives in their converted horse trailer with two ponies and a dozen chihuahuas.

"Breeding stock," they reply in unison to my question, with a tone that rebuffs any further queries.

This is the lair of the synanthrope, creating community on the edges of public order.

"Patrol One, Quinsam Five. Moving on."

THE PATIENT SOIL

"He's... over there. That man, he's..." puffed the stout matron—blue hair, red smidge of lipstick, a dusting blush of rouge. My first concern was she might expire on the spot. Wheezing and bending at the waist, she dismissively waved me off, pointing with a gloved hand in a noble gesture toward the end of a laurel hedge. "Go, go."

As a city gardener in Victoria's flagship Beacon Hill Park, I came across some pretty bizarre objects and had been an inadvertent witness to equally peculiar acts. Druggies, hookers, pervs, drunks and other modern species of degenerates all enjoyed the democracy of the common lands. One fine afternoon in early summer, I looked down from pruning the rose arbour and saw a pile of lumpy grey powder. I stirred it with my boot but found no clues.

"Oh, that stuff again," said my boss. "Look around the edge of the park." He pointed with his clippers, an extension of his own arm as they usually were. "See those apartment buildings fulla old folks? Retirees, refugees from Winnipeg, living out their days shuffling these paths, *clackety clack* with their walkers." He stopped and seemed to remember he'd be there one day, too.

"So, our trees, shrubs and flowers give 'em some sorta peace. And when they croak, many of them have no relatives nearby, no one to come and deal with the body, so they get cremated. And then a friend hobbles out here some evening and dumps Martha or Clarence in the flower bed. So, just work it in. Good for the roses."

I thought I'd seen it all. But now, summoned by the matron, I trotted around the end of the hedge, ready to defend the park. What awaited me stopped me dead in my tracks.

There, in the middle of a large planting of zinnias, marigolds and sunflowers, stood a frail, elderly gentleman wearing a neat blue blazer of appropriate cut and weight for the season, an old school tie, knife-edge grey trousers and polished oxfords glinting in the sun. He held his cane reversed, the crook down like a golf club. With each step, he swung it to the left then to the right. Step, swing, step, swing. Each arc severed a half-dozen plants and a rainbow of flower-heads went flying.

You don't drop an old legionnaire by a quick shot to the nose from the end of a handy tool, as might be the case with other rowdies, so I yelled. He looked up with watery blue eyes. One cloudy, the other clear.

"Just come on outta there please, and whaddya doing, busting up all those flowers?"

He walked like a man condemned, stopped in front of me, raised his head and looked me over, turned his stooped shoulders and looked at his path of destruction.

"Why? You really wanna know why?" He lifted an arm and extended a bony finger from a splotched parchment hand toward the foliage. "'Cause they're so young and beautiful and I'm so old and ugly. That's why."

In a month, new ashes. Dig him in. Say goodbye.

LITTLE HABITS

Max and Seal Boy sat in the crew lunchroom chain-smoking. Ruffling through the drifts of ignored paperwork on my desk, I wondered what collection of humanity would show up for work on this grey and drizzly Monday.

The country was immersed in an alphabet soup of make-work programs: LIP, STEP, EBAP and OFY. It was like a gold rush: think up any vaguely beneficial project, put in a proposal, and the money arrived. The only hitch to this largesse was the requirement to hire the unhireable—the junkies and drunks, the slackers and ne'er-do-wells. My task was to shepherd this motley gang, instill some manner of work ethic, and usher them back to productive lives, whether that was their goal or not. All in twelve weeks of pogey cheques.

We were hand-building recreation sites and fire trails with the Forestry Department. No power tools for these guys. A chainsaw in the shaky hands of a crackhead coming down off a weekend binge is a fearsome sight best avoided.

Slowly they straggled in, these half-dozen men assigned to my care. Unshaven, sallow and scrawny, they slouched around the table sneaking furtive glances at each other and at me. I began my orientation talk knowing full well that most of them were still out in their private wonderland. As

I droned on with the required sermon, my new crew either nodded off or squirmed. Seal Boy sat quietly humming and rocking.

"Please leave your jugs, bottles, fixes, snorts and bongs at home. Tomorrow, when you show up, try to be dressed for the work."

It was November, getting cold and clammy in the woods. Several of the crew had only thin sweatshirts or jackets. Most were shod in scuffed runners, some with no socks, no hats, no gloves, no rain gear and no clue. The program bought them work clothes, but many sold or pawned them off for crack or wine and still showed up half-dressed. Luckily, I had an overflowing box of left-behinds from previous trainees.

I rousted the crew and we piled into the crummy and drove to the work site. Max and Seal Boy were rare indeed since they had chosen to work together through another program cycle. Max was a tall, gangly junkie, but like many of them, he was a paradox. With dark eyes crackling under a load of opiates, he could quote obtuse and archaic philosophy to rationalize his obsession.

Once and only once did I err in judging Max. "You're a smart enough guy," I said. "How come you're shooting up all the time?"

A flat smile tightened his thin lips. "We all have our little habits." He picked up his shovel and walked away, leaving me to think about the thin line between routine, custom, habit and addiction.

The new crew had been on the job for nearly a month when Seal Boy went to the hospital. He had passed out while tending a pile of burning brush and toppled into the fire.

Luckily, his sodden wool duffle coat protected his body, but his face and hands were blistered. Max took the accident hard and went into a black, frightening sulk.

Despite this, the gang was shaping up nicely. Getting these guys out of the halfway houses and fleabag hotels and into the clean, green woods worked wonders. I had no illusions about miracles, but was heartened at the end of every day when another hundred metres of trail was built, and the tables, rails and an outhouse went up in the rec site. Every Friday afternoon I brought in pizza and pop to go with their methadone. They began to joke with each other and smile with rotten teeth. Maybe it was just my fantasy, or stubborn hope, but some of them seemed to stand taller, meet my eyes, put a bit of extra effort into their labour.

Near the end of their program, I arrived one morning to find Max ashen and shaking outside the door. I thought this was just the residue burning off, but he grabbed my arm and told me to follow him.

Over the years we had found many strange objects in the park: boxes of accounting ledgers, a pail of dead hamsters, bloody clothing and discarded appliances. I feared Max had found—or was a party to the depositing of—a body. But with his breath steaming behind him, he charged fearlessly down the trail.

On the weekend some road warrior had gone on a four-wheeled rampage through the park, smashing the rec site. He was neither bright nor probably sober since his macho truck was firmly and definitely stuck in the mud where he had tried to plow through the stream. The winch cable was still attached to the uprooted trunk of an ornamental

Japanese black mountain pine the crew had struggled to plant on the hillside above the rec site.

Max stood beside me, quivering with rage. At the sound of a profanity, I turned and saw the rest of the crew up on the roadside looking at the mess. One by one they picked their way down the hill with their impatient tools in hand and joined us. No one spoke.

Finally, Max turned to me, swallowed hard and said, "Why don't you take a long drive down to the other end of the park for an hour or so?" His black pupils were pinholes of fury.

I started to speak, thought better of it, and simply turned and walked away. As I got in the truck, I heard the first smash and tinkle of glass and smelled burning rubber.

The crew was finally taking pride in their job. The program had worked.

NIGHTINGALE

Every seventh wave is supposed to be unique. Every set of seven then should be exceptional. Seven times seven, seventy times seven. I give up counting and just sit on this log watching them, listening to the hiss and rattle as the waves tumble up and down the gravel beach. But I'm still waiting.

We moved to this remote island in late spring when the blue-eyed Mary and sea blush were blooming and hopeful. No one seemed to know who owned the decrepit cabin, so Troy mumbled something about the Common Law Right of Occupation and moved us in—him, our two kids from previous lives and me four months pregnant, just over the grumpy pukes. I have to hand it to the man, he knows how to make do. He sawed a straight-grained red cedar log into fragrant blocks, split them for shingles and fixed the leaky roof. Some flotsam plywood became shelves and a tabletop.

After living on brown rice and oysters for weeks, he said, "Screw this," and took off in the boat with the last of the gasoline. He'd always come back in a day or two with useful stuff—a generator, a new Honda outboard, crates of canned goods. I never heard the details, but I did reap the benefits.

I put the kids in their bunks and sat by the window beside the kerosene lamp, reading *The Dharma Bums* and listening to the propane fridge gurgle and belch. The radio batteries were fading so I rationed them like a wartime housewife. The trees swayed with the rising wind and before long there were whitecaps in the channel. Troy wasn't born a sailor, but he had a pretty good hand on the tiller and more than once brought us through some nasty circumstance. I got up and stuffed another chunk of driftwood into the stove and watched the sparks snap and crackle up the corroded chimney pipe.

Must be something I need in men: this innate ability to scrounge, to survive by any means necessary. My first husband had a night job driving a truck for the Sally Ann, going around the sleeping city to the donation boxes and retrieving the goods. He skimmed off some of the really cool stuff and brought it back to our hippy ghetto in Kitsilano where we lived in the furnace room of a big old house just off Fourth Avenue. He was Robin Hood to the squatters and strays of the neighbourhood. They came running to see what booty they could claim—funky clothes, carpets, fiddles or antiques. Now here I was, waiting through this southeast gale for another benevolent thief.

Under morning's pink cloak, I heard the whine of an outboard coming into our bay. Sure enough, Troy was soon dragging the dory onto the beach in front of the shack. He looked all excited and wound up. Maybe he outran the police boat, like Robert Mitchum in the old *Thunder Road* film from the fifties. Or maybe he found a big box of cash so we could get off this rock and into a decent house with more than a rain barrel for water and a pit for a toilet.

"Guess what happened. You'll never believe this."

By now the kids had crawled out of their musty sleeping bags and stood in the doorway rubbing their eyes and blinking. I hoped the story had a happy ending.

"So, I drift into Cocktail Cove real quiet just after sundown. Tie up to a tree and go to that house on the point. Didn't see no one around."

"Anyone," I corrected. "Didn't see *anyone* around."

He hates it when I do that, but I can't help it. Just sounds so white trashy the other way. There are other things he does that conjure up that ratty single-wide outside of Cache Creek where he grew up with four brothers and sisters. Like leaving his bootlaces loose through the eyelets so he can slip the boots on and off easy. Clumps around like an old movie monster.

"Okay, whatever. Anyway, I go up to the house and the door's unlocked. No lights on I could see. In I go and start looking around until I hear this sound. Music. A guitar being played really quiet in another room. Song sounded really familiar. I step around a corner and the floorboards make a squeak and this figure gets up from a big ol' chair. And guess who it was?"

"Santa Claus? Huckleberry Finn? Frida Kahlo?"

"No, smart-ass. It was Joni Mitchell herself. All blond hair and cigarettes. She stood there looking at me an' me at her. No one said nothing."

"Anything. No one said *anything*."

There's lots of stuff about him I don't like, and he feels the same way about me. One night after the kids were asleep, we were sitting around the candle playing checkers with black and white beach pebbles on squares he etched into the plywood table with his fish knife. Somehow, we got into saying, "Another thing I don't like about you..." First him, then me, then what I said reminded him of something and he'd go off, back and forth until it went from mean to petty to ridiculous to comical and then we were both laughing and holding hands over our mouths to not wake up the little ones.

"Jeez! Gimme a break. So, I said to her, 'I like your music.' That's all I could think of. Original, don'cha think? And she smiled that lopsided way like on her album cover and asked me what I was doing in her house. What could I say—that I was there to take whatever wasn't nailed down? I told her again that I really liked her music and wanted to meet her."

I moved over to the stove to stir up some oatmeal for the kids. Troy certainly did like her music and I remember someone saying they even heard her on the CB radio, which we used to communicate around the islands. Everyone has some ridiculous call name. Troy's was Ace of Spades. He said hers was Nightingale.

"She never asked me how I found her hideaway. Maybe when you're a star like her nothing's surprising. But here I was—just her and me. She made a pot of coffee and we sat around talking. Then all of a sudden, she gets up and says it's time for me to leave. It was midnight and blacker than coal outside so I thought that was kinda strange. Rude, even. But then, seeing as how I was there to rip her off, I suppose I couldn't really talk about manners, eh?"

I ladled oatmeal into the chipped bowls and opened up a can of peaches from the box Troy brought in from the dory. He had obviously visited a couple of other cottages before the Nightingale's.

"I started out the door, thinking I'd just sleep on the floor of the boat until early light. Then she says to wait a minute and I hoped she'd changed her mind. But she went back into her cottage and came out with a guitar. 'Wouldn't want you to go away empty-handed,' like she knew for real why I was there. She asked if I played and I said no, but my old lady does. So..."

Troy lifted a gunny sack and pulled out this incredible guitar, all inlaid with fancy bird's-eye maple and mother-of-pearl, iridescent and watery like the inside of an oyster shell. I stood with my mouth open, took the instrument and gave it a soft strum. The strings seemed still warm and the curious tuning proved it was indeed hers.

All summer I made melody for the family, for the shaggy sheep, for the pleasure of cove and sea, for the beauty of song, and for the baby curled in my womb. Could have sold the instrument and lived for a year. Maybe when bleak November comes, we promised.

But when the nights lengthened and the raucous cranes flew urgently south, a candle tipped and our shack burnt to the ground. We all got out but lost everything else, including the Nightingale's gift.

We found a house on another part of the island, abandoned by discouraged back-to-the-land amateurs once they found out how hard their perfect lifestyle really was. And we're still waiting on the baby (if it's a girl, we'll name her Joni) with only my voice, my singing to bring it home. But I miss the twisted arbutus tree with the kids' tire swing slanting over the clamshell beach. I miss the scampering feral sheep with their tousled dreadlocks. I miss the deep green quiet that filled my heart when it'd been days since anyone had come by.

I'm here waiting for that special seventh wave to bring it all back.

BURIED ON PAGE FIVE

Later in the evening, just before last call, Vic looked up and said, "Know what our situation calls for? Some dead cops." This got the attention of the rest of us at the table, made Louis the bartender scowl and raise an eyebrow. Lucy, the server with the dragon tattoo encircling her neck, stopped with her precariously balanced tray of beer and stared, not only because of his words but also the slow, level manner in which he spoke. Everyone else in the wharf-side pub turned to look at Vic. The rumble of voices paused to hear what was next. Vic was well-known for his often entertaining, sometimes offensive rants against the logging company that keeps us employed. We waited.

"I mean, look at this," he said, oblivious as usual to the stares. "This here..." and he stabbed a stubby finger at the newspaper he was reading. A bit disappointed, people returned to their serious drinking and the background hum resumed.

"You want some front-page coverage, nothing beats a cop-killer story. Makes the headlines for weeks. Like this one in Toronto who got killed by a barefoot nutcase driving a stolen snowplow. Not making light of him getting run down or nothing, but you know how many cops marched down Toronto's streets for his funeral? A thousand! Not only other city cops, but Mounties on their horses, border guards, ambulance drivers in yellow reflective jackets, and state troopers from across the line with their Terminator shades and brown stetsons."

His eyes followed as his finger slid across the page and thumped here and there for emphasis.

"But this is the best yet: there was even CN rail cops and, get this, parking enforcement staff. The meter maids. At the risk of annoying someone, I got nothing against respect, but jeez, who gets it and who don't? That's my point."

Gusty rain beat in from the Strait against the streaked windows facing the bay. Vic spread his big hands over the newspaper, looked around the pub and, with an exaggerated sigh, shook his head and continued.

"If a man gets killed wearing a cap and badge, flags 'cross the whole country are lowered for a week. So wearing a uniform and a wide gun belt when you go down makes you a hero, but if you're wearing Stanfields, Carhartts, a hardhat and packing a lunch pail when you breathe your last, be lucky to make page five of the news."

We knew what he was saying. Last winter, just before shutdown, a company crew boat was pounding into rough seas up Knight Inlet headed for a ten-and-four camp shift. Ten long days in, four short ones out. The tide was flooding against a miserable outflow wind and the standing waves built up huge. Once you're headed up Knight, there's no refuges, no safe coves, only the sheer granite flanks of that unforgiving fjord.

They figure the boat must've been going full speed when it came down hard on a big hemlock deadhead lying low in the swells. The boat broke in two, threw everyone overboard, and sank in half a minute. Vic's brother and uncle were on board, with four other guys. Water in the inlets is icy runoff, thick and opaque as mother's milk with glacial sediment—sand and gravel slithering in from the Klinaklini and Franklin Rivers. What goes in usually sinks fast and stays down, the ancient grey silt filling pockets, closing eyes. Wearing heavy boots and bush clothes for their workday on the sidehill, they had no time to grab for life jackets.

Reporters came and got their close-ups of strong men swallowing hard and blinking fast, women holding each other up, kids hiding behind legs, saying, "Where's Daddy?" Long shots of the foggy bay. They sat at our kitchen tables and we told them things into their microphones. Close things. They turned off the cameras when these got too hard so we thought they understood.

But a couple days later, four Mounties get gunned down by a madman in a frozen Alberta barn and the live feeds and satellite trucks couldn't get off our island fast enough. The drownings were forgotten. Old news. They were just loggers, not headlines.

Vic leaned back in his chair, lit a cigarette, sipped his beer and said, "More than twenty men a year die in the bush. No flags, no parades. Maybe what we need is something like dead cops."

HOUSE, WAVING GOODBYE

Peggy craved solitude the way cracked earth yearned for rain. It had been twenty years since Vince died in the logging accident that changed her life with the snap of a rusty cable. She had tucked that moment and all the rest deep inside where she carried her misery until, like her milk cow, it was digested and passed. But for a couple of months after his funeral, she was reminded of her loss daily, by every truck going by hauling logs, gravel, shot-rock, or Vince's co-workers heading for the sidehill. The drivers yanked on the lanyard in the cab and the airhorn blared a *toot-toot* salute, often startling Peggy from her much-desired numbness. Leave us alone, leave me alone.

The settlement from the company paid off the mortgage on their eighty acres and her widow's pension stretched to make do for the rest. She raised their kids as best she was able, taught the boy how to make lump-free gravy, gave the girls her two housekeeping secrets and showed them how to hammer a crooked nail. Job done, she thought as the youngest one was prodded out and she set to emptying his room. She liked the hollow sound of the bare walls—no bed, the utter lack of clutter, no race car posters, just faintly dark patches on the walls, unbleached by the sun. The rug lay rolled up, all lumpy in the corner like a badly made cigarette. Just her and a resident mouse tolerated by the old cat, who was in turn accepted by the old dog.

On the kitchen wall hung a Co-op Feed Store calendar on which she noted her few appointments in red pencil. Days with something written in made her uneasy, the time and occasion glaring at her as she passed by, reminding her of the part other people still played in her life. She liked to walk through rooms talking aloud, leaving half-finished conversations hanging like fly strips stuck with fragments of sentences she'd pick up on her next circuit.

Tuesday. West Valley Women's Club—joined many years ago when her life was full of noisy children, when an escape for an afternoon of quiet conversation and rummy was somehow refreshing. But now, with her days so blessedly replete with nothing, the banter seemed trivial and forced. She had somehow managed to escape hosting the event despite the hints and thinly veiled jokes about her solitude.

With no kids and no man to clean up after, Peg dressed how she wished. Most days one of Vince's baggy plaid work shirts hung loosely and comfortably on her. Old clothes were one of the few reasons imaginable why she would ever seek the company of a man again. The fabric was worn cuddly smooth by his travail and even after many washings she thought there remained a lingering, contented musk.

Vince, she sighed, and turned to other matters.

Peggy would have given away all her plates and cutlery but one of each, except for the weekends. Oh, the weekends, and the holidays, laden with expectation, with history.

As much as she appreciated the well-meaning deluge of her kids, their spouses and her grandchildren, she quietly looked forward to the last taillights winking down the drive. Family time was possibly overrated, she thought. So much activity in the old farmhouse knocked her off her equilibrium. She became lightheaded, as if something had consumed all the oxygen in the room, like the dead rivers near factories she'd seen on TV. So much talk as each person tried to outdo the next in the latest bout of sibling rivalry. At longed-for but rare pauses in the banter and bragging, she threw out a word or two about her own life, admittedly plain and unadorned by desire and design compared to that of her spawn. The pack jumped on it like hounds to a bone, then quickly carried the conversation back to their own frenetic schedule of activities. Her ears rang until Tuesday. She felt like a planet with too many moons tugging at her, making her wobble on her axis, perigee and apogee all confused. They had taken over; she was just along for the ride.

Saying goodbye took forever. After several hours of admiring pictures of porridge-smeared fat cheeks while thundering feet surged through the house, she rocked forward on her chair, looked optimistically toward the door, slapped her hands on her knees and said, "Well..."—sometimes more than once—willing that no one would toss out a memory or a boast to start a whole new line of conversation. They'd say goodbye in the living room as they arose, hope fluttering in her ample chest like a moth around the yellow back-porch light. They'd say goodbye in the kitchen as she edged toward the screen door. Then halfway across the porch they'd stop again and take one last bellow at each other, showing grin and gullet, door open, letting in the cold in winter, mosquitoes in summer.

It took hours for her cat and dog to emerge after the last car door slammed, last horn tooted and all were gone. The barn animals had escaped to the far ends of the fields to stand under the maples a safe distance away, keeping a wary eye on the riotous house. For their salvation, she had told the small children about the farmer in Oregon who was eaten by his own pigs, creatures the neighbours said he had loved.

At the last gathering, she sat on a straight-backed chair as chaos churned around her. She noticed a fly crawling across the windowpane and willed herself into it, imagining what the room looked like through its multiple eyes. Could each segment look at one member of her family singularly, isolated from the pandemonium and diapers?

She thought she knew her kids well enough, but they still surprised her. Connected by the womb common to them all, they often seemed unable to accept their dissimilar emotions, expectations and achievements. Her eldest daughter somehow married a Pentecostal and learned to be shocked by her mother's uncensored words.

"Maybe I should go to town and find some cowboy, get lucky and knock the dust off my old kewpie."

"As if," snorted her youngest girl, the one with so many rings in her ear she looked like a spiral notebook. Thumb rings on stubby fingers and of an age where every response required sarcasm.

The newly holy-roller daughter heard worse growing up, but feigned dismay at both of them, possibly for the sake of her white-faced husband, who stared at his clasped hands.

Peg remembered the wedding reception, years ago, with a tectonic fault line drawn down the middle of the rural hall. On one side his family, nursing the bottle of free wine. And on the other side, her rowdy cousins and relations who quickly polished off the freebie, bought a dozen more and sat around getting drunk, talking about the last time they sat around getting drunk. Same old, same old. At some point that night she realized she was more than a bit tipsy herself. Before her loosened tongue betrayed her, she made a few abrupt farewells and stumbled across the parking lot to her pickup, oblivious to the whispers.

Without being fully aware of the miles and minutes, she had rolled into her farm lane and sat in the truck listening to the radio fading in and out, and the cooling tinkle of the engine. She didn't take to booze like some. Her uncle was a classic functioning alcoholic, somehow managing to keep his job as an insurance agent in town while drinking morning, noon and night. He often mocked his brother, her father, for not joining him deep in his cups, and she hated him for that.

Booze disturbed the balance she so desired and that night was no exception. There was a moon behind thin clouds. She slumped her head against the cool and reassuring window; it was what she needed. Morning found her with dried spit in the corner of her mouth, her patient old dog waiting, wondering and wagging beside the truck.

Six weeks later, Peg held a fat parcel just arrived in the mailbox. She slit open the flap and pulled out a stack of pictures from the wedding. When she had been unable to avoid the hired camera, she had quickly looked at something to one side, as if what she saw was infinitely more interesting than leaving a good image. In every photo she appeared in, her image was blurred, out of focus, ghost-like.

After a quick glance, she slid the pictures back in the envelope. What to do with them? So many of her women friends had elaborate albums, well organized, with photos labelled, dated and named. In addition, the pages were stuffed with letters, programs, bulletins, pressed flowers, scraps of fabric and prize ribbons. Mementos of what had been, what was past. Dates when long-gone relatives would have been a hundred years old, but still dead all the same.

Why? Were they so afraid of disappearing into the dust that swirled off the country roads, slipping down some sad, imagined slope into oblivion? They spent endless afternoons poring over pages they had examined countless times before, as if the images would age and change like the subjects, and they lived in fear of missing some moment. They hummed and *awww*'d at each page, murmuring platitudes like "Family is all there is," and "I just live for my kids." They'd receive new photos and treat them like sacred relics, staring at them reverentially and expecting others to do the same. Stare and stare, searching the small faces for vestiges of satisfying resemblances that meant so much.

Jeez, Peg wondered now, as she crossed the living room, thinking back to those more social times. What about your own dreams, your own private visions behind your eyelids? Don't you know our kids will grow up and forget us just like we did in the sixties, with our long hair and beads? Only now it's dreadlocks, pink like cotton candy or blue as a urinal puck, a face full of metal and tattoos like a sailor. Why would she want to spend her time keeping track of all that when she could just live her own life? She thought she might be lacking some piece of the puzzle, some fragment of heart necessary for a mother.

And what was missing in her that she kept her shelves and mantel uncluttered? Her wedding photo, once coloured but now fading into monotones, one or two of the kids in sports or band uniforms; that was it. She figured what they were today, their successes and failures, marked the passage of years better than framed diplomas and other dust catchers.

But there was one icon she cherished above the stark austerity. It was a ceramic animal made by her boy in his elementary school art class. To her it resembled an armadillo, though she had never seen one in real life. He dropped coins in it through the slot in the top, calling it his piggy bank. Pig, not armadillo, he insisted. After he moved out, she picked it up and was impressed with its heft, then noticed there was no hatch or way to retrieve the money. Other than a hammer, she thought, amazed it remained intact through all his teen years.

Only later would she notice that below the eyes, her son had carved two small tears.

So Little Pig merited special treatment. In the mornings she set it on the windowsill facing the sunrise. By late afternoon it was in shadow so she moved it to the west bay window. She found a box of stick-on googly eyes in the back of a drawer during one of her periodic purges of clutter. After she stuck them on where the pig's carved eyes were, she noticed they seemed to follow her throughout the house. Now she never felt alone rattling around the gaunt rooms.

It was early fall. The maple and alder leaves turned colour and fell, having done their utmost to nourish the trees that summer past. She felt grateful to them for their temporary beauty, somewhat envious that their contribution was so obviously fulfilled while hers was grudgingly ongoing. She welcomed the change of seasons and autumn's moist, earthy smell. There was easiness in her mind as she thought of the lengthening night and more reasons to stay in bed under fluffy quilts.

The wood stove squatted black and ponderous in the front room. The stovepipe bent into the brick chimney and carried away the smoke and sparks as it had every winter. The heater had been Vince's domain. He was almost religious about stoking it with bone-dry cordwood seasoned for at least a year in the shed. Hauling the ashes, cleaning the soot from the stovepipe—his rituals. She managed, but without the zealous diligence of her late husband. In recent years she let many such daily tasks slip without notice. Dog hair chased the dust bunnies and the stove choked and smoked. A few sparks popped like mini meteors through the front grate left ajar, but they usually blinked out before hitting the worn floorboards.

She was in the barn pitchforking manure into a wheelbarrow, a task in a place of great solace, the smell of warm cow, the dog's straw hollow, the darting swallows swooping into their mud nests in the rafters. But weariness overcame her and she lay down on a pile of fragrant hay. It seemed her eyes had been closed but a moment when the dog's barking and then the cow's bellowing awoke her. Still dozy, she lay with her eyes on the cobwebbed beams, calling to the animals in a soothing voice to no avail. She sat up, brushed the hay from her wool shirt (his wool shirt) and looked at the fidgety animals.

Stepping out of the barn door, she stood with her mouth agape. Flames were licking out every window of her house.

The glass heated and shattered; floors collapsed. All she could do was watch. She spotted the cat walking across the driveway—she probably should have worried about the cat.

She found her garden bench and plunked down. Red and orange fingers pushed through the dry cedar shingles and waved. The house was saying goodbye.

Half an hour later, when the roof had fallen in, she rocked forward, slapped her hands on her knees and said, "Well, job done," and called her dog. She felt cleansed. But still, she already missed Little Pig.

DITCH CLOTHES

"I'm really tired of seeing all of those types everywhere I look," Marvin Chesterman proclaimed to no one in particular and everyone in general as he wove through the maze of mahogany desks to his private sanctum. The floor-to-ceiling-windowed corner office overlooked the harbour of trollers, gillnetters and sailboats with their halyards slapping aluminum masts, for which his insurance agency collected premiums for disasters no client ever hoped would happen. But, fortunately for him, it happened often enough to give him a tidy six-figure income, a rural acreage with an equestrian centre for The Wife, and his cherished BMW classic roadster.

"I mean, they're everywhere. On every street corner, bus stop, camping in the city park and especially outside that hippy grocery store two blocks over. They must take shifts, move from town to town so no one recognizes them.

"Coming in this morning, get this, there was this old raggedy geezer with a stick collecting cans along River Road. Probably for booze or drugs. But what gets me is down in the ditch was this little girl tossing empties up to him so he could put them in his sack. Not only returnables, I can see that. But everything. Worthless garbage. Litter. Who knows what else? She must have been only ten or twelve. I mean, what kind of life is that?"

The morning sun had been in his eyes as he slewed the roadster through the maple-lined curves, enjoying the feel of its engine through his right foot. He was almost alongside the pair when the child in the ditch tossed a Lucky Lager can that skittered onto the pavement. The BMW crunched over it, flinging it up into the wheel well with a bang.

Marvin had slammed on the brakes and jumped out, crouching to look for damage to his exquisite automobile. Finding none, he turned to stare at the man and girl. They were too far away to make any recognition or to yell. He shook his fist and drove off with a squeal of the Michelins. Glancing in his rear-view mirror, he thought he saw the old man writing in a small notebook. Taking down my licence number?

Finally in his quiet office, he closed his door and went to the window. On the dock below gathered the annoying crowd of wharf rats, a scruffy group whose boats bumped against the wood timbers and rarely went to sea. A floating slum, he called it.

They're everywhere.

Only a few weeks before, he had harangued the town council to enact a bylaw about transients and beggars. At each meeting of the chamber of commerce, for which he reminded others that he was past president, he sought support for his cause. Smiles and nods but no action. Yet.

Then it got personal, with the old man on the road this morning.

A fine summer day, a little breeze off the bay, a few puffball clouds easing across the sky. With the sharp tang of tree sap from the sawmill wafting through an open office window, Marvin settled into the day at his executive desk.

Midmorning, he left the office to grab his usual mocha at the coffee bar down the block. Taking his first sip from the steaming cup, Marvin heard music and looked across the street. A tousled young busker with a guitar played old favourites to a small gathering of tourists.

Harmless enough, he thought. Happy, entertained people buy souvenirs and meals as they stroll. At least that guy was providing a bit of service for his money. Not like...

His gaze shifted to the sidewalk next to his office. In broad daylight sat the old man from the ditch line. Alone. No delinquent can-throwing child. His head was down. Sunglasses, ratty jacket, no socks. Scuffed mismatched shoes. Even Marvin's horse-barn clothes were of better quality. A grimy ball cap with a few loonies lay on the sidewalk in front of the bum.

For what? Not music, not a thing. He doesn't even look up. Is that a smile or a smirk? Getting something for nothing. Marvin made a wide path around him, like he was afraid something evil could leap out and soil his crisp Dockers and polished wingtip Northampton brogues.

Too close, he murmured back in the office. Opening his email, his calendar reminded him of the noon chamber of commerce luncheon. How convenient. He was still steaming about the panhandler, the little girl and the wharf rats.

At midday, he slipped on his well-fitting Harris tweed jacket, a prize from the Provincial Underwriters Association honouring him as best salesman of the year. He stepped onto the sidewalk, quickly glancing to see if the vagrant remained. No. He sighed in relief.

Entering the hotel's meeting room, he felt at ease with the affable companionship of car dealers, store owners, building contractors and guests. Proud, successful people. His peers. They had guts and gumption. He liked the way that phrase rolled off his tongue. It would make a good slogan when, not if, he decided to seek elected office. He built his castle in the clouds as he made his way to a table in the middle of the room and sipped at the complimentary glass of light white wine. He chatted with his tablemates until the president tapped his glass for attention.

"Members and guests. It is my pleasure to welcome Dr. Dick Benson, the new dean at our local college. As a newcomer to our town, he will provide a fresh outlook on familiar things we may have overlooked."

A round of applause while Dick Benson stepped to the lectern. Marvin, who had been chatting with the owner of the hardware store, turned toward the head table and choked on his wine.

Dr. Dick was none other than the can-picker, the panhandler on the sidewalk. Couldn't be, Marvin thought, with watery eyes and reddening face.

"Thank you for the invitation and the welcome, on behalf of myself and my wife, Karina, and our two children. Katie, who is twelve, has a school project researching the waste stream and the types of refuse tossed along our roads. I help her now and then. Karl, fourteen, hopes to be a classical musician and is playing his guitar for the public. My undergrad work was in business and economics, but my doctoral thesis had to do with urban sociology. What makes a town like yours distinctive? How do the residents treat each other?

"Like a hunter entering new ground, I have enjoyed observing local attitudes, unnoticed by those being observed. I try to do this from varying viewpoints and personae. Again, like the hunter, I wait and watch, remain camouflaged, stay in the shadows. And this I did before accepting the position at your college.

"Why, you might ask. In the early 1950s, in our neighbour to the south, a white journalist wanted to get a real sense of what it was like to be a black man facing hatred, Jim Crow laws, and the loss of the civil rights we take for granted. Like eating in a restaurant, attending a movie, buying a home, voting, or running for political office. Simple acts like quenching your thirst at a public fountain on a steamy day in Alabama. The journalist was nearly killed several times when, with his cosmetically changed new skin colour, he crossed the racial lines. He later wrote a seminal book, *Black Like Me*.

"While privileged men and women like ourselves will never experience such discrimination, there are many in our community who do. Often it has little to do with such a blatant factor as race."

He paused for a moment to let the words sink in. Marvin slumped lower in his chair. He wished he was near an exit, not in the centre of the room. He knew what was coming. He'd heard it all before.

"I did some sampling of demonstrations of helpfulness and of prejudice. I am pleased to say the former surpassed the latter by a wide margin. One factor, which has been noted in many jurisdictions, not just yours, is that philanthropy is disproportionate to wealth. In other words, judging by surficial indicators, the more money one has, the less likely one is to share it with those that don't."

Dean Benson went on to describe some of the situations he gathered his data from— asking a stranger for help, entering a nice restaurant—with slides showing graphs of how people responded, based on how well-off they appeared. Thankfully, there was no mention of the roadside incident.

"This has been true for as long as we have had civilization, and probably before that. But to be fair, the opposite is often true. Two millennia ago, a wise and compassionate man said to those who would hear, 'The poor you will always have with you. Therefore, I command you, 'You shall open wide your hand to your brother, to the needy, and to the poor in your land.' The lesson? Look not too far afield for the opportunity for goodness.

"Thank you for your time."

The chamber president stood up to acknowledge the dean.

"We sponsor major projects in the developing world. Water wells, latrines, schools for girls. As a matter of fact, the spark plug behind many of these is here today. And he has an item of business he wishes us to consider. Marvin has brought to my attention an issue somewhat related to Dr. Benson's remarks.

"Marvin Chesterman, stand up." A ripple of applause rose.

Trapped. He rose, nodded, and plunked back down. A silence hung in the room as the audience waited. And waited. Finally, Marvin waved his hand dismissively.

"Still working on it. Needs... uh... more study."

Later, after all the chamber business was finished and the wine glasses refilled, the crowd milled around in small circles of interest. As he tried to exit gracefully, Marvin found himself shaking hands with the new dean. Before hope of anonymity could even flutter in his chest, the speaker smiled.

"Nice car. Nice shoes."

BEYOND YUQUOT

No one wants to turn their kayak and head back. But we have been paddling for eleven days on the west coast of Vancouver Island, riding the swells over nightmare shoals, and are desperately low on supplies. Dry clothes are but a memory, and the aroma rising when we pull off our cockpit covers is staggering—smoky wool and stale, wet neoprene, pungent seaweed, the unmistakable musk of sleeping bag romances, and the rapidly decomposing leftovers of what little rations remain: rye crisps that are anything but crisp, tea bags used and reused barely colouring already tannic outer coast water, and all the rolling papers stuck together in a long accordion spliff.

Even so depleted, nobody is ready for land—the lure of the ocean rising thus strong. The hypnotic staccato *tappa tappa* of the bareback corduroy sea ripples beneath the eager boat. As we make night crossings holding Polaris on our right shoulder, below us luminous streaks reveal the passing dart of sculpin and flounder. Hawaii over the western horizon seems within reach and quite reasonable. We are addled by saltwater, so like our own blood.

Seated snugly in a boat, we are more of the water than on it—akin to the sleek otter whose supple curlicues we envy. On the sea for so long earth feels foreign when we go ashore on rubbery legs. Out of the kayaks we are inelegant, naked and slow.

Three stay on the narrow fringe between ocean and hemlock to set up camp. The rest scatter in search of protein. Some drop handlines into clean water and sit motionless as beach herons, twitching the bait to tempt the wily codfish and salmon. Others scramble onto black headlands to pry gooseneck barnacles and sweet orange-meated mussels from the shattered rocks where sea and continent so fiercely embrace. A crab trap loosed from the deck of a kayak disappears with a hopeful gurgle into the dark and deep fronds of a seaweed forest. Whoops of delight echo as bounty is reeled in.

From all points of the compass we return to camp. The beach crew followed deer trails up the nearby creek to a patch of salmonberries to gorge and gather. We are cousin to buck and bruin.

The feast begins. Driftwood-fire-barbequed salmon, colourful cod and mussel kebobs, crab steamed in a kelp-lined pit, and the sweet meat of roasted barnacles slurped; salty chin juice worn like a feral badge. Cavorting around the flames, we dance catastrophe and rapture. Last night out. Beyond Yuquot.

DONKEY SHAME

She was dependable in her need of him twice a day without fail and he to her in promise and practice. Ed Miller leaned his cheek against Cupcake, their Jersey cow, and listened to her four stomachs gurgle and rumble as she digested the hay Ed's wife, Willa, forked into her manger. The cow's neck bell tolled softly in a familiar tone.

The barn was stuffy from the August heat. Morning light slanted through the gaps between the cedar shakes on the roof. They twisted and cracked as if trying to escape the oncoming cudgel. Chaff floated in the stillness like aerial plankton. Summer flies bumped dumbly into the single small window at the far end of the barn, the glass nearly opaque from cobwebs waving in the wing wash. Ed felt like he was next to a living, breathing furnace. Squeezing each teat gently, he heard, without looking, the steady stream filling the pail—each pull raised the tone a note or two. The cow stood placidly, as contented cows do, flipping her tufted tail in the dexterous manner that often amazed Ed: bugs, an itch, or just a mischievous joke when she slapped him alongside his head or dipped into the milk pail. She knew how to smile.

"Nothing decent or good ever comes down from Campbell River," he said, obviously continuing a conversation he was having with himself while milking.

Willa stuck her fork into the pile of sweet-smelling pasture grass, took off her headscarf to wipe a runnel of sweat from her forehead.

"Now, what is that supposed to mean? You still stewing about that baseball game? I know they are everybody's favourites, but the Comox Valley Kings were soundly whupped by the Campbell River Tyees. Fair and square."

"You all stick together—"

"Oh, so it's about my relatives up there, is it? Keep up that attitude and the cow'll hold back her milk," she said with a laugh.

Ed grunted, shrugged his bare shoulders under his grimy overalls and stood up. Carrying the milk pail, he turned toward the barn door.

"Not so much. Even if they did have a big parade with the trophy like it was the frigging Stanley Cup. Island Champions 1938. Hooey." He jerked his head around. "Now this."

Stepping out of the barn, he looked north and pointed his nose into the breeze. Willa had often said he used his nose to point at whatever he was talking about, be it an absent person, the weather, politicians, bureaucrats, looking upward to a benevolent or vengeful deity.

Dust devils spun across the barnyard as the hazy red sun poked over the few trees remaining around their farm. For a moment he thought the dingy taint was from the hundreds of clearing fires smouldering in the rural areas, his included.

They had been on these forty acres of logged-over, burnt-off, stump-ridden rock pile for sixteen years trying to make it into the farmland they were led to believe it would be. When he was demobilized from the army, he and other survivors had the "opportunity of a lifetime" to become landed gentry in the mild climate of Vancouver Island. Ed and his new Vancouver wife soon realized it was more a program to keep the ex-soldiers occupied while the Dominion shifted to a peacetime economy, not needing the skills of jobless uniformed men well versed in shooting and high explosives and susceptible to the Bolshevik propaganda attracting the idle. Ed and Willa worked through the seasons, digging and hauling endless tons of stones, blasting the rotten stumps of the old-growth forest, piling and burning day and night. Smoke was a constant reminder of the task.

But this time it had a heavier heft, a pitchy, almost kerosene weight and power in it.

"Now this," Ed repeated and spat into the dirt. It was so dry his spittle raised a puff in the grey ash at his feet.

But no one grumbled about the heat and dust. Loggers' wages were low in these Depression years, but more than the tin-canners' pittance paid for sitting in the shabby relief camps up at Oyster Bay. All through the early summer of 1938, the crews felled, bucked and yarded the immense fir and cedar in the Comox Valley. They took only the best portion, leaving behind the tops, limbs and lesser trees shattered by the last descent of the ancient forest. The debris was so deep that a logger could work all day, scampering over the slash, and never touch ground. Prime logs were money and times were tough.

The steam donkey engines hissed and roared ash, the cables yanked taut pulling the giant timber to trackside. The mainline, thick as a man's wrist, ran from the spool winches up through the pulleys rigged high on the topped spar tree above the sweating crew and stretched out into the clear-cut, waving in the heat. The cable drooped to the ground and sung through dry duff and over glinting exposed granite.

The weather turned hot early in June and the wind blew steadily from the northwest. The crews left their bunkhouses before daylight and worked until the fevered heat drove them back to camp, leaving behind one man as a firewatch—a token response to the rudimentary provincial fire regulations.

Sitting in the shade of a tall stump, the watchman passed the hot afternoon, sipping at his jug of water and humming a popular Guy Lombardo tune. Late in the day he arose and, walking by the towering deck of logs, stopped and sniffed. Smoke. Before the crew had gone, they'd pulled the coals and embers from the steam donkeys and trackside loaders and left them cold. But the smell was not the acrid scent of a doused firebox, but of fresh and hot burning resin.

He moved around the pile and saw the first tongue of the dragon flickering through the shimmering heat of the devastated forest. Breathing in the freshening early evening wind, the beast grew before the man's eyes. In a matter of minutes, the smoke became flame, the dragon inhaled and gave its first roar, and the log deck erupted. The firewatch stood with his ineffectual backpack "piss-tank" then ran for the little two-man gas speeder waiting on the rail siding.

After the barn work, Willa washed her face and hands in the tin tub, patted some water on her sticky neck. Then she sat on the front porch snapping beans to can up and watching a few vehicles roll past on the unpaved road, raising even more dust. To her surprise, several of them were military trucks full of people, mattresses, crates of chickens, boxes with sleeves dangling out in the wind, obviously packed in a rush. Though she did not recognize any faces, their plain clothing and scads of blond children spoke of the Mennonite settlers living between them and the Oyster River. She offered a wave but there was none returned from the solemn adults. They just stared back the way they came, straining to see what was left behind.

Ed joined her and watched the procession.

"Funny, eh, with the events unfolding in Europe and Mr. Hitler, how we can have a bunch of German-speaking people right here. Mind you, they do keep to themselves. And some of them work for the King of the Comox Valley, Bob Filberg, at Comox Logging Railroad. Good workers, so I hear. Work ten hours for eight hours' pay. Also heard they won't sign up for army service if war breaks out, as some say it's bound to. And I heard—"

"What's funny, my dear husband, is how you manage to hear all this, but can't hear me when I ask you to take off your boots outside."

Ed smiled and looked again at the road.

"Where they going, I wonder? Back to the home country? That'd open up more jobs for us real Canadians."

"Maybe to town for the weekend. Market is this Saturday, they'll have lots of vegetables to sell. But, no, you wouldn't take your mattresses for a weekend. Which reminds me, did you fill the boiler with water, like I asked, so I can get these beans done? If you managed to hear me in all this dust and heat. I have a bushel of tomatoes to put up as well. Cukes to pickle. Never stops, this life of a country gentleman. The kids'll be home from school soon, too, and hungry as raccoons."

A truck pulled off the road and into their yard. A family was crowded into the cab, and the back was piled with household goods. Steam leaked out from under the hood. A big-boned man leaned out of the cab and waved a saucer-sized hand.

"Speaking of which," Ed commented, as if Willa hadn't even spoken, "that's Peter Friesen, one of the churchy types from up Black Creek. His farm is the closest one to us, just past the big wetlands and cattail ponds. More rocks and swamps. What they didn't foist on us, they sold to the Mennonites."

"You sound like those old men in town, their days spent airing grievances for all and sundry."

"Pete works for Iron River Timber across the Oyster River. He came into the shop at Headquarters Camp a while ago needing some repair work done on a rusty old one-lung Easthope engine. You've heard those single-cylinder engines thumping by on fishboats."

This time, his nose directed Willa east toward the beach and the Strait.

"Told him I'd have to work on it on the sly—Hardass Jack McKenzie, he'd send me down the road if I used up company time fixing something for a Kraut. Then I'd be home underfoot every day. You wouldn't like that, now." Willa gave him a swat with her dish towel.

"In a week or so, I got it running sweet. But after, he said something I couldn't understand. He paid up and said, 'Donkey Shame,' or maybe 'Donkey Shine.' I didn't get it. You know how noisy it is in the shop. Maybe I'll have to ask him. Seems kinda rude to make a point of their poor English, though."

"Well, here he is now."

"Good day, Mr. Miller. Mrs. The truck has boiled dry almost. Need to fill the radiator, if you have some water for me?"

"Sure, Pete. But if you pour cold well water in that blistering engine, you'll sure as hell crack the block. Good timing. Just got some hot water on Willa's stove, which I'm sure she won't mind sharing with you."

Ed walked into the house and returned with a pail of hot water. "Say, what's with all the traffic coming down from your area? Not all moving back overseas?"

"No, we are being told the big fire is getting closer and bigger. So, we have to go to Courtenay into a camp set for us and others."

Ed looked again to the north, from where nothing good or decent came.

"What about your farms, the livestock and such?"

"Each family took only a few things. I let my cows and chickens out to run. They are in God's hands now," he said with a sigh. "The house, the barns, too."

"Jeez, man, that's bad news. Say, if you want you could bring them down here. Surely the Forestry can stop it before it jumps the Oyster and it's a good ways still to Merville proper."

"That is very good of you but it's too late now, we must keep moving." He filled the radiator, climbed into his truck and said something over his shoulder, then drove off to join the sad procession.

"There, he said it again. 'Donkey Shame.' What the hell is he talking about? Making a joke about the steam-pots in the woods, or some jibe about our horses? I mean, didn't we just give him water to get that old truck to town? And offer to hold his animals?"

That evening, ash and fine bits of burnt twigs began to swirl like unseasonable snow into their farmyard. The sunset took on an ominous hue as the roiling plume filled the sky. Scorched leaves wafted down to cover the blooming hollyhocks and nasturtiums. Ed decided to bring Cupcake and the two beef steers into the barn. He heard them snorting and banging on the gate, so great was their inborn fear of smoke. The pigs in their outside pen ran in circles grunting. Ed threw them a bucket of oats that they, un-piglike, ignored.

Before he went to bed, he stood at the window. The smoke was underlit orange and seemed closer. Reminded him of the flash of artillery his regiment faced in the muddy fields of death in France. The kaiser's gas, guns and steel, then. Now, twenty years later, the same knotted guts. But here he was giving water to Germans and offering help.

Once he drifted into a thin blessing of sleep, he thought he heard a truck heading toward the fires, then large animals pounding past. But worry and fatigue pulled him down.

Since moving to Merville, his life had settled into a reliable pattern. Eat, work, sleep. Sundays go to St. Mary's and then a bit of socializing and visiting the afternoon away. But come night, his mind took flight. His dreams had always been vivid, almost tangible. Fantastic creatures and unusual, impossible situations played movies on his eyelids. Tonight, they were fierce and unsettling. Donkeys with red eyes and flaming manes tore through with hooves like steel, striking sparks as they ran.

Willa shushed him and rubbed his back to stop his thrashing and moaning.

Ed jerked up in bed and looked out the dark window, then to the ticking clock on the table. The livestock had bellowed and kicked all night but seemed quiet now. Fuzzy-headed, he tried to make sense of the time and the dim light.

Eight o'clock. Should be full daylight. Jeez, I really slept in.

Up, dressed, then peering into the gloom.

"Great God Almighty. Willa. The fire. It's nearly here!"

They hurried down the stairs. The house reeked with eye-stinging smoke. The scene from the front porch was unbelievable. Less than a mile away, on the far side of the bullrush and swamp grass wetland, flames roared, pushed by a stiff wind. From the north, Ed thought. Nothing good.

"Get the kids up and dressed. I'll check on the animals."

He ran across the yard and stared at the barn. The stall doors lay in splinters, demolished by the panicked cattle. He stood dazed, not knowing what to do next. He flung open the gate to the pigpen and the pigs bolted into the smoke and disappeared. Ham already smoked, he thought.

Smoke and ash limited visibility but Ed heard a motor coming toward them, coming from the direction of the flames and destruction.

A familiar truck rattled into the farmyard. Peter Friesen stumbled out, his face blackened and his clothes dirty and smudged. Several other men stepped stiffly from the truck box and lifted out shovels and buckets.

"Pete, you coming or going? Hard to tell with all this muck."

"Last night some of us snucked past the guards on the road." He gave a small smile. "We have lots of experience getting past soldiers in Russia."

"So, we go to my house and save it. You saved it. So we come back here to save yours, Ed."

"Whaddya mean, I saved your place? I never left here all night."

"That engine you fixed last month. We hooked it up to a water pump and kept all the buildings wet from the pond and hoses. You did that. We would've burnt out."

Ed scuffed his boot in the dirt, unsure of what to reply.

"Well, I... uh... How did you find your way here this morning? Can't see ten feet."

"Your cow guided us. And our cows, she saved them too. Listen."

The unmistakable tinkle of Cupcake's neck bell rang through the smoke. Soon she came trotting into the yard, leading their steers and several of Peter's Holsteins, bits of mud and bog mire stuck to their underbellies.

"Would you look at that! She must've led them into the wetland for the night, now she wants milking. Hey, old girl?"

While they were talking, Peter's men had unloaded the blessed engine and pump from the truck. Quickly they ran hoses out to the pond and started spraying water on all the buildings. They threw shovelfuls of dirt on the rain of sparks, burning twigs and branches. Ed's kids ran back and forth with wet rags, swatting any sparks that landed on the house, barn or woodshed. The shower of fire driven by the blustery gale seemed endless and the pond was draining rapidly. Soon the pump would be sucking mud.

Then, in an answer to prayer, the wind began to blow from the south, pushing the fire back onto its own scorched path to smoulder. Within a couple of hours, the danger was quenched and the exhausted men slumped to the ground. Willa brought plates of bread and cheese. Jugs of cool water quickly drained into parched throats.

Ed sat on a bench and looked around him.

"My farm is safe. Yours is too. Cows need milking. Everything suddenly seems ordinary again. Thank you, Peter."

"No. *Danke schön*, Ed."

"Okay, what does 'Donkey Shame' mean, Pete? What's that got to do with any of this?"

Peter gave a huge laugh.

"In our language, Plattdeutsch, it means thank you."

Willa looked at Ed. "Who's the donkey now? Go milk Cupcake."

Ed grinned and pointed with his nose.

"See that, Willa? Wind's coming from the south now." He stooped and picked up the tin bucket. "What did I tell ya?"

ALL THE BEARS SING

Smoke lies thick in the valleys. The hills are afire. I make the rounds of the backroads and bush campsites on Vancouver Island looking for new burns and errant campfires.

As I bounce along a logging road near the end of a long and dusty patrol, I spot someone standing with his thumb out. Hitchhiking is unusual here, far up this potholed mainline, twenty kilometres off the nearest pavement. I hiss a sibilant "Whatssssup?" and my ever-present companion, Duffy, lifts his head. Riding shotgun in the pickup, he doesn't miss much, so the quiet whisper brings his ears to full perk. Nose aquiver, brown eyes bright and searching, he stares through the bug-splattered windshield at this scrawny creation of a man.

I rattle to a stop beside him. He looks at my truck with its provincial Forest Service crest and takes a step back. Despite my greying grandpa beard, a diplomatic demeanour and my most reassuring Smokey the Bear grin, he flinches at the sight of a crisp tan shirt and badges. But reassured by the dog—everyone likes a dog—he leans forward again. He looks like a cross between Captain Jack Sparrow and Huckleberry Finn: scrawny, knobbly knees poking through holes in grimy jeans. Untamed blue eyes glint from under a slouchy sombrero. His fingers patter on the roof of my truck.

"C-C-Can you give me a ride? My name's C-C-Corey. I live up the road a ways—off the Rossiter Mainline." He gives me a prolonged look, gazing with such urgent intensity, such burning expectation. I hold my breath. The hound watches warily; nostrils sift for clues and find much to consider. "Can you? Will you? I've walked from town. No one's stopped. Why? My name's C-C-Corey. It's a good name."

His sentences clatter like rocks in the rusty wheel well of an old truck climbing a loose gravel road. A few words tumble out, then they stall, spin and roll back down to make another run. Some more verbs and nouns roughly seek form and purpose. Eventually it all takes shape and he breathes a deep sigh, worn out by the effort.

"Can you? Will you?" He waits.

There are no houses hereabouts, only exuberant young plantations, rough haul roads, splintered clear-cuts still shuddering from the yellow machines. Nothing I would call a home. Curiosity fills me, so despite regulations, I agree, pull over the attentive dog to make room, and off we go.

I drive my fidgety passenger along the mainline then up a steep, rutted spur road to where an old teardrop trailer is perched. Perhaps it was once the pride of a suburban family on summer holidays, doing the slow haul over mountain passes behind the sensible four-door sedan, headed to sunny lakeside parks beneath cinnamon-barked pines. In its past it may have smelled of buttery suntan lotion, campfire smoke and burnt s'mores; now it is Corey's home high above the Rossiter.

"How did you get it up here? I'm impressed!"

He seems evasive yet eager and proud. "My cousin has a Free Miners Licence and a truck. This is on his claim. I'm legal. Believe me. It's so perfect."

His haven is close to a rollicking creek at the edge of a large clear-cut where ten-year-old fir seedlings poke through the endless billows of purple fireweed swaying in the breeze. He has a safe fire pit, a neat stack of cordwood, the ground is swept, and there is no garbage. He hunkers like a folded jackknife and rolls a smoke from a scant bag of crumbled tobacco scavenged from the abundant butts littering the sullied earth in the squats and unofficial campgrounds.

"I'm never leaving. It's better out here than..."

I notice some letters on a battered lawn chair. He sees me looking at the envelopes and quickly whisks them away. He holds them lightly in his fingers and slowly shakes his head. He is about the same age as one of my four sons, born with a soft and clean heart, but dealt a rougher hand. And though obviously self-reliant, he's delicate, almost fragile. I get an avuncular urge to watch over him.

"I just don't belong there." He points in the general direction of settlement. "All the rules don't make sense and no one else plays by them but they expect me to."

He offers to make me a cup of tea, but stops halfway into the trailer and instead pulls out his guitar to play a song he wrote. "Do you know the wind through the pines makes different music than when it blows through the alder and aspen?"

After one strum he pauses, distracted again, and sets his guitar down gently on the gravel to tell me about his neighbours, the bears. "They sing each night when they come down the gullies to drink at the creek."

"They sing? What do they sound like?"

"They go 'gronk, gronk' in deep grumbly voices. Eight came by last night. I don't fear them. Or the wolves or the cougars. I'm more scared of the weekend party boys and their jacked-up trucks. Drunk and dangerous. I go hide."

Looking over the nodding brush in the late afternoon sun and feeling the warm outflow wind, I envy him sitting there alone and quiet, listening to the bears crooning as they amble languidly through the dusk, gronking anthems of praise for abundant berry crops, for joyous couplings in mossy boudoirs, and the resulting comical cubs.

He glances at me with an earnest, almost confessional scrutiny.

"I shit on a log by the creek and then wash it away, but the other day I forgot and when I came back the next morning there was a shrew chowing down on my business so I watched him for a long time and named him Drew the Poo Shrew. D'ya think it is okay to shit in the creek if I am feeding Drew? I only eat mostly grains and what I find in the bush, no bad stuff. Is it okay? Is it, Mr. Ranger? Is it?"

Seven days later, I return on patrol to Rossiter Mainline, anticipating seeing Corey again. I'd been carrying him in my heart the past week. There is a twenty tucked in my shirt pocket and a box of garden veggies and venison steaks behind the truck seat for him. But around the last corner I am disappointed. The trailer is gone, somewhere up the tangled lacework of logging roads. Corey, lost in his own maze of isolation, burdened by noonday demons, moved on like the hot, dry wind through the waxy leaves. Now who will listen to the bears or the singing of the aspen? Duffy follows his quivering nose to the creek but no Poo Shrew. The patrol seems much lonelier now.

Smoke fills the valleys. The hills are afire.

LIPSTICK

I'm standing by my green government truck fourteen kilometres from town. Down the hill comes an old four-door sedan—a real land barge from the seventies, once proud in the country club parking lot, now just rusty and faded, sagging under a load. I wave it to a stop and the driver, a weary-looking woman, nervously glances at my Forest Service badges. I am surprised when I have a quick look inside the spacious interior—all the seats but hers are removed and the space is piled high with fir and alder. The trunk lid flaps, unable to close for the burden.

"Uh, do you have a firewood permit, Ma'am?"

"I got a kid. No money. How am I supposed to keep my house warm? Tell me that."

"Well, this wood is cut and split by someone. Gotta cost something."

She grabs a quick look in her rear-view mirror and, with a sigh, gives me a tired smile. "I can pay you like I paid them."

"Them?"

She jerks a thumb backwards and I turn to see an equally decrepit one-ton truck rattling down the mountain with two men in the cab. They stop a ways back and wait and watch.

"How about it?" she asks again. "Trade? Five minutes of your time? Maybe ten. Depends on you. I can put on fresh lipstick. I can say that I love a man in uniform."

"Just go." I send her on her way.

The truck rumbles toward me and doesn't intend on stopping until I stick out a hand. No licence plate, stacked full of fresh-cut cordwood. The driver resembles a depraved Grizzly Adams—wild hair, a snooze-stained bushy beard covered in wood chips, little pig-mad bloodshot eyes full of anger. The scrawny man on the passenger side keeps his eyes on the floor, clutching a Timmy Ho's coffee cup. He's still breathing hard.

I repeat my question and step back.

"No, I don't have no fuckin' permit and if you're smart you won't fuckin' be here when I come for another load. Wanna do something about it right now? I'm ready." One hand goes for the door, the other reaches deep under the grubby seat.

A feeling comes up as the truck motor ticks over. My wife once asked her tai chi mentor whether her learning martial arts would save her in an attack. Henry's response: "You must learn to listen to yourself and *not* be in a place where such a one can approach."

Aware of my being very alone and far from any help, I reply, "No heroes here," and move farther away. "Have a nice day." He stares at me a moment, perplexed, the sizzling challenge draining from his face, the opportunity stolen. He spits out the window and drives away, flipping me the finger solely on principle.

OVERBURDENED

Garba slouched over the red railing of the government wharf, picking at the peeling paint as she watched Lonnie's snub-nosed barge scrunch onto the clamshell beach. A venerable maple leaned over the foreshore with branches holding broad leaves like palms upturned in welcome. The front ramp of the barge slammed down to unload the vehicles on board.

In a cloud of blue diesel exhaust a shiny new Land Rover bumped ashore pulling a tandem trailer loaded with plywood, two-by-sixes, sacks of concrete, rebar, boxes of nails and bundles of shingles. The driver looked cautious.

Spewing gravel from tires so unblemished they still bore the little rubber whiskers from the mould, the truck engaged the All Wheel Drive Quad Track Positive Grip function to grind three generations of barnacles and whelks into oblivion. Garba only had a glimpse of the people in the vehicle, but she knew there'd be time. It was a small island and only one road headed up the hill from the wharf. Everyone would eventually know all about them, just as every resident knew all about everyone else.

Spitting a loose shard of tobacco from her rolled smoke, she headed toward the small store/coffee shop/pub at the land end of the wharf. Facetiously named Red Tide Seafood

Ltd., it was *the* dependable source of news and rumours—the fount of all knowledge, some might say. As expected, the locals were all watching the parade. Bosko, the often-intoxicated skipper of the small ferry servicing Pyrite Island, Gordon, a high-liner cod fisherman, Ted and Monica, the store owners, Roger, who owned the island's only bulldozer, with an attitude to match, and a few other woolly citizens.

"Must be the people who bought the old farm at Linton's Beach. A hundred and fifty acres waterfront. Lotta bucks, I bet."

"Some land pimp made a sweet commission on that deal."

"The old house isn't worth much, though. I mean, it was derelict when we squatted there our first winter on the island," Garba remembered. "Mice everywhere in the walls. Insulation was sawdust and rodent shit. Still, it was better than those shacks and hovels when we moved out onto our own lands. Alder poles and vinyl tarps. Twenty ways to fix oysters and brown rice. Still can't stand them."

"They don't look like they're gonna use the old rat castle," Bosko opined. "Could nearly see the L.L. Bean tags on their clothes, and Lee Valley on the tools. Nice to see a better class of people coming than..." He stopped short of more detail.

Monica chipped in with her initial observations. "At least they don't have mullets. Mullets mean trouble." Everyone nodded in agreement.

When Wes Graham, a noted small-time felon, inherited one of the old houses from the cannery days and invited his scruffy mulleted friends from the mainland to visit, there was a plague of missing generators, tools and outboards.

Break-ins increased. (More like walk-ins as no one had door locks—or even doors, in the case of tipis, yurts and wall tents.)

Such petty acts were tolerated until they escalated into an influx of bikers, parties, hard drugs, turf disputes and the sudden disappearance of Brother Allenby, a self-defrocked monk whose sackcloth robe was cinched by a very ecumenical display of objects and symbols, druidic, pagan and Gregorian. Each finger was encircled by papal ring replicates. A gentle man who may've simply been an unfortunate witness in the wrong place at the wrong time.

The front door made its unmistakable screech, and everyone turned their heads like a flock of ducks watching a swooping eagle. One of the recent arrivals strode in, faced the tables and grinned.

"Good morning. Name is Derek Martin and we just bought..."

"The Linton's Beach homestead," Garba said. "We know." Derek's grin went through several possibilities as if unsure which was appropriate.

"Welcome to Pirate Island," she continued, breaking the silence. "I'll introduce you to this bunch of layabouts and tell you who you can depend on and who'd be taking a risk." Nods of polite acknowledgement followed her finger, the nail painted pink with sparkles. Names and nods.

Introductions over with, Derek asked, "Uh, you called it 'Pirate Island' but the papers say 'Pyrite Island'?"

"Oh, that's just the official name. When most of us moved here thirty-some years ago..."

"Forty-two," corrected Gordon.

"Me, was more like thirty-nine."

"I was three when my parents bought their fourteen acres on Randy's Road, with four others who've since moved on. Do I get to add their time to mine?"

"Seventeen."

"Born here, moved away, then back. Does all that count? It ought to." Bosko always tried to get in the last word.

Garba returned her attention to Derek, who looked confused at this litany.

"So... the name of the island?" he asked hesitatingly.

With a comforting smile and soft voice, like she was describing the origins of the universe to a seven-year-old, Garba began her explanation of the nomenclature.

"When the first wave of us longhairs came here, full of *Whole Earth Catalogue* ideas and tattered copies of *Walden*, *Desolation Angels* and *Raincoast Chronicles 1* and *2*, we wanted to enhance and romanticize our idea of the island as the last refuge for scamps, scoundrels and unrepentant misfits looking for treasure. Only it later lived up to the more realistic 'a beautiful place where good marriages come to die.' But by then the name had stuck and since then it's been Pirate—at least to us, the socially marooned. And it's annually renewed by CRAP."

"Treasure? CRAP?" Derek asked.

"Oh, the Committee for Resources and Planning."

"The local government?"

This brought a boisterous hoot from the patrons. "Such as it is. Sure."

"But still elected?"

"Naw, acclaimed by consensus."

"Well, that is commendable, these days."

Bosko seized his chance. "Consensus just means keep

talking until you see it my way. That's not so commendable, is it? Talk, talk, talk."

Garba glared at the skipper but offered no rebuttal. It was a familiar conversation. "I'm the Queen of CRAP. It's a dubious honour. A few of us step up to help run things. If someone else wanted to do the work, they'd be more than welcome to."

"Pirates, rogues, hidden treasure. Unelected anarchy. Sounds like an interesting place for us."

Bosko blurted, "More fuckin' RRRUPS. That's all we need."

"Which are?"

"Rich Recently Retired Urban Professionals. Lot of your types come here, all 'back to the land but with five hundred grand' and an attitude that matches their patches."

Garba reminded him most everybody came here from somewhere else.

"Not me! Goddammit, I was born here! My afterbirth got buried under a fir tree at the home place."

Roger laughed. "Last time you said it was an apple tree. Anyway, it died."

A horn beeped outside and Derek turned to go, but paused at the door.

"My types? I'm just a retired geologist. I've known many who spent their whole lives looking for treasure on beaches, river banks or in hard rock. Most of them were deluded by a glint on the ground, chasing a sparkle at the end of the rainbow that turned out to be only common iron pyrite. Fool's gold."

Derek smiled. "Happy to join in on the metaphor, me buckos. See you around."

A week later the barge brought another load of building materials. Because the tide was only starting to come back in, Lonnie couldn't get far enough up the beach to unload directly into the trailer, so the newcomers had to pack all the boards and sacks of ready-mix cement across the sloppy foreshore. Lonnie had to keep nudging the boat in to match the rising water. With more freight to deliver elsewhere, he urged the small crew to hustle. Then, ducking inside the cabin, he grabbed his radio mic.

Within ten minutes several battered cars and noisy trucks pulled onto the wharf. A dozen men and women, naked toddlers and several dogs immediately sorted out the situation and formed a line from barge to trailer. Derek stepped aside and drooped. The cargo was quickly unloaded, and Lonnie cranked up the ramp, beeped his horn and with a frothy wake headed out. On time.

Garba sat on the log next to Derek and simply said, "Pirate style. Let's go up and have a cold one. You buying?" Without waiting for a response, she headed for the pub, leading the mud-spattered and thirsty mob.

They filled the tables amid the nautically themed decor—fish floats from boats sunken or abandoned, nets hung with collected flotsam and crustaceans, the smell of dried-up carapaces—and the beer was quick to arrive. The first bottles went down with a sizzle, allowing those following to cool the brains for more profound considerations.

"We looked all around the Linton house and decided it was too far gone for renovation," Derek's wife, Linda, said. "We haven't even been able to stay there, it's been the tent for us so far. Friends are bringing us a loaner camper on the weekend. As for the house, we're going to deconstruct it."

As usual, Bosko flared. "That's a heritage building. What makes you people think you can just come in here with your million bucks and change everything just to fit your vision."

"Deconstruct? You mean demolish it?' asked Gordon, ignoring the rude outburst.

"Yes, but with some care. And help. Most of the structural boards are still sound. Beautiful knot-free old-growth fir. So, anyone who wants to pull nails can have all they want. For free!"

Free. The magic word.

The deconstruction started the next day. A half-dozen of Derek's friends came over on the day ferry and joined in. Hammers, crowbars, chainsaws and many hands. The sound of nails reluctantly releasing their eighty-year hold on the tight, pitchy grained studs, joists and rafters was like fingernails on a blackboard. Only when a saw hit a hidden spike did a voice curse, causing everyone to stop and look, expecting blood.

Four days later, the house had miraculously vanished. The unusable wood was piled in a stack for a bonfire. Even the ground was raked, and dragged with a magnetic bar, picking up errant nails and other metal.

Giving the old bones a few days to recuperate, Derek and Linda put out the word for a bonfire party and potluck, for visiting friends and locals alike.

As the sun slipped behind mountains to the west, cars and trucks rolled down the hill and kayaks, canoes and dories slid onto the beach. Small fishboats like Gordon's dropped anchor off shore.

A vast assortment of food was displayed on the plank-and-sawhorse tables. Potato-and-leek casseroles, baked empanadas and exotically spiced veg dishes. Pork, beef, venison and feral mutton for the unrepentant carnivore, and tongue-curling sweet desserts to satiate the blind munchies. Kids chased the dogs. Dogs chased the kids.

The feast took a new twist when the grannies started seriously drinking homebrew ale and overproof fruit wine. They sniffed the dishes, searching for the mystery seasonings. It was competition at its most subtle.

At dusk, the fire was lit and the brittle, dry wood shot flames into the evening sky. Mason jars were refilled with homebrew and the musicians opened their instrument cases: a pair of guitars, a five-string banjo, a stand-up bass, accordion, fiddle, an ocarina and a valise full of harmonicas. For percussion, various hand drums, a washboard with finger cymbals and a well-pummelled red cedar beat box.

Not surprisingly, Garba took the lead. She first nodded to Derek and his crew.

He stood up and said, "Most of you were pulling nails with us and met us. But Linda and I want you to know how much we appreciate all of the help you have been, and that we are making a commitment to this land and to this island. And to the communal spirit you have embraced. We're looking forward to getting to know you and fitting into your community of pirates." He returned to his stump and Garba stepped forward with her fiddle.

"Howdy, you all. We're the Has-Beens, three Bean sisters and some Wanna-Beans. I'm Garba Bean, to my left is Joanne, then Gwen, and over there, that long drink of water on stand-up bass, is Steve—obviously not one of the famous sisterhood, but useful in his own manner. Let's get going!"

After a bit of twangy tuning up, they launched into a set of old favourites—folky, bluesy, "Country Roads" imbued with an afro-reggae beat, then a vaguely Slavic tune with modal chords droning to the drums. The pace accelerated easily and an inspired couple leapt onto a table for an improvised Cossack dance. Cheers and clapping encouraged them. The dishes were cleared and soon a conga line formed to weave through the tables and benches, sweeping up more dancers. All of Derek's group were grabbed and joined in. The line grew and stretched, then snapped its tail, sending younger dancers laughing and rolling in capoeira moves. Those of longer age landed with a groan and took a bit more time to arise.

The music and feasting continued deep into the night. As the stars replaced the pink and salmon sunset, Garba and Linda sat on a log, listening to the peaceful lapping of small waves.

"So, I guess you're going to start building right away? Lots of good workers and equipment available."

"Building?" Linda reached down and grabbed some sand, let it run through her fingers. "Not exactly. But I think what we are planning will be a surprise to all."

"Ooooo, how mysterious!"

"As might befit a pirate."

Life slowed to a late summer lassitude. Gardens, both visible and covert, were tended with diligence. Only a slight breeze ruffled the drooping leaves of the alders and maples. Houses became too hot for sleep. Outdoors, hammocks and foamies were draped in mosquito nets. Ponds dried up and water became precious. Everyone sniffed the air for the worrisome scent of smoke.

    Bosko tossed in his bed, unable to sleep. Doris, his wife, lay bare and snoring open-mouthed beside him.

    He left the clammy bed and walked down to the dock with a cold beer in his hand. The ferry bumped against the creosote timbers, still sticky from the day's heat. He went aboard and lay down on one of the fibreglass benches. Dozing fitfully on the hard surface, he heard the deep thrum of a large towboat. Wanting to know about all passing nautical traffic, he got up and walked to one of the salt-spray-glazed windows.

    Blinking again, he made out a silhouette against the first tinge of sunrise. A castle had just disappeared around the rocky point at the entrance to the harbour. A castle, complete with a steep roofline, gable end gargoyles, two round turrets and what looked ever so much like a dragon. Sure, he'd been at the pub until closing time, but this was no barley illusion. But by the time he sorted out his location and stumbled onto the dock, there was no sign of it. No castle, no dragon. He considered firing up the diesel to pursue the phantasm. But what if nothing was there? What if something was?

    Making the next morning's scheduled crossing to the big island, he kept his eyes on the horizon for the nocturnal illusion. He had always been a lucid dreamer, so he wondered if this was a mirage carried across the thin separation from reality to fantasy. It was driving him so crazy he nearly forgot to cut the throttle coming into the marina on Vancouver Island. Only the shouts of angry yacht owners roused him from his puzzlement.

    Who could he ask without sounding like a batshit crazy old drunk? Who would keep it in confidence? There was only one, his biggest critic and favourite confidant, and he looked her up as soon as he returned to Pirate Island.

He met Garba at the pub in a corner table where he whispered his vision.

"A what?" she exclaimed. "Castle? Dragon?"

Bosko nodded. Roger burst in on their conclave. "Holy shit, you'll never believe what I just seen anchored in Linton's Cove." Not waiting for an answer, he waved his arms excitedly. "A barge with a big old house on it. They're gonna need my Cat to pull it up onto the land. They also have an excavator. Ever too awesome."

"Yeah, we already know. Came in last night. Probably waiting for tomorrow's high tide," said Garba, watching Roger deflate. Enjoying every minute of it. Bosko sat openmouthed, in a way relieved that his vison was real, but also disappointed he was not the bearer of the news.

The cove was soon packed with curious islanders. The word travelled faster than a flu bug through a bunch of snotty-nosed kids at the school. The barge bobbed with activity as the workers affixed cables and timbers under the house.

At high tide they slowly began to slide the structure ashore. Roger's dozer and the excavator strained the thick wires humming tight, and with a creak and groan it all worked like it should.

Derek stood on shore with his arms crossed, watching it all, and smiled as Garba walked over to him.

"Mickle Brothers have done this lots of times," Derek said.

"How? Where? Why?" asked Garba.

"Got it cheap in Victoria. Was going to be demolished for a condo tower in James Bay. They said it wasn't heritage worthy. Ridiculous. Look at those turret windows. The small flat roof with the wine-glass railing was called a widow's walk, where women could look to sea, waiting for their men to come home. Or not. Beavertail and diamond shingles. Fretwork gingerbread on the porch posts. This was a skilled tradesman's home, not some tycoon or lumber magnate. So, we bought it and they moved it. Now it's here. Pretty cool, eh?"

"Immensely so."

By the turn of the tide, the new old house stood where the original Linton farmhouse once had. The movers loaded their backhoe, coiled up the lines, shared a beer with the spectators and slid back into deeper water. With a toot and wave, the tug mumbled back south.

Over the next month, workers swarmed Linton's Beach. Foundations were filled with dozens of wheelbarrows of concrete. Once the footings cured, the house was lowered into place, swaddling like an old hen over a clutch of eggs. Another milestone. A neighbour's tractor and a drag harrow smoothed all the ruts and gouges, which were then reseeded. With all this activity, Derek was looking exhausted. Sweat and dirt stuck to his salt-and-pepper beard. He took every opportunity to slump on a stump in the shade and stare at the house.

Garba suggested he slow down and take it easy. Go on island time.

"Once the seeding is done and the roof's weatherproof," he replied. "It's September and you know the rains could start any time now. You just never know what's coming. And I want to be prepared."

Indeed, the air now had an early autumnal flavour.

There had been a few light showers, adding dampness and the delicious relief of dirt washed from appreciative trees and shrubs. Around several old farms were several heritage orchards—a testament to the foresight and faith of the earlier islanders. Often neglected and tangled, some were being brought back by careful pruning and mulching. Northern Spy, Broad-eyed Blenheim, King, Bramley's Seedling and Ellison's Orange. A homestead in the centre of the island had an apple press and neighbours brought crates of fruit for juicing. Gallons of aromatic amber cider poured into jugs and bottles.

Several steam canners rattled away over an outdoor fire. Jars of the nectar lined up for processing. Lids pinged as they cooled and sealed.

Everybody had to sample each batch. The drunk wasps added a touch of danger. Tastes ranged from puckery tart to smooth, rich sweetness. By evening the squitters were a common affliction of the over-indulged. Some won; some didn't and left in a rush. Evening and sweet applewood smoke drifted through the knobby old trees. The buckets of spent pomace were loaded in a pickup for a pig farmer. Soft guitar music lifted from bacchanal-slouched bodies. To Garba, it felt absolutely medieval.

Two months later, the last of the maple leaves had fallen and Derek and some islanders sat on the deck of the restored house, admiring the view west toward Vancouver Island. Like an old Chinese woodblock print, the mountains receded range beyond range into the haze. A gentle southeast breeze nudged the passing weather up the Strait.

A small cruiser named *Serendipity* dropped its anchor offshore and lowered an inflatable dinghy with a splash. One man stepped in and rowed to the beach.

He had a face tanned by outdoor work and an open smile. In the dinghy lay a faded and worn red vest with many pockets full of instruments and dangling fluorescent flagging tape. He carried a folder of papers and a rolled-up map.

"One of you must be the landowner? Nice place."

"No one can own the earth; we only borrow it for a time," Garba replied.

"Yes, I suppose in a way that's true. But some of our species doesn't see it that way. I guess I fall somewhere between those two poles. My name is Dan Lawrence. I'm a geologist with Brookfield Mineral Enterprises."

Surprised by the coincidence, Garba merely said, "And what is a geologist interested in at Linton's Beach?"

"Simply, what lies beneath our feet. To most folks, geology may seem a dry and static science, but it's fascinated me for years. This old earth is alive and roiling, only to a very different schedule than us—or even the old-growth forest, what there is left of it."

He paused and looked down at the pebbles at his feet.

"What do you see? All these various colours, shapes and patterns. Coming from different parents, so to speak."

"Sounds about right for this island. Confusion on Father's Day," Bosko joked.

"Yeah, and that's what makes my job so interesting. It's like a mystery hidden deep from our sight, and it's been there waiting for five billion years."

"Waiting? For what?"

"It would be the height of hubris to think that it's expecting us, humans being such recent arrivals. I like to believe it occasionally awakens with a yawn wider than we could ever imagine, stretching out its kinks with a strength so powerful it folds stone like fabric, squeezing coal into diamonds and tearing kilometres-thick rock like paper, mixing and churning as it rouses. Magnetic forces, physics beyond our puny boundaries. That's my job, looking for it. Like trying to find a pearl in one of the oysters around this cove."

Everyone sat spellbound, looking at the rocky ground in new wonder.

Finally, sporting a scruffy salt-and-pepper beard, his hair dirty from digging septic lines, a rumpled man stood up behind the others, stepped forward and offered his hand. Dan looked at him, surprised at his dishevelled appearance. "Derek Martin, UBC grad in Earth Sciences, 1982. Retired here forever."

Now it was Dan's turn to stand open-mouthed, before saying, "Not only a grad, but post-grad with honours. Your picture is on the wall outside the dean's office. Magna cum laude. Industry grants for research. Now here you are, a fellow mining geologist."

Garba and Roger looked at Derek with unbelieving expressions.

"You're one of them?" Roger asked.

Derek paused for a moment and took a deep breath.

"Yes and no. I mentioned that I was a geologist but retired. My research was on mine reclamation and mitigation techniques. Cleaning up what the industry creates. You may've heard of the Mount Washington open-pit mine? After the mining company extracted all the economically accessible ore, they filed for bankruptcy and walked away. The acid mine drainage ran into the Tsolum River, wiping out historic salmon runs for a couple of decades. I worked as a consultant for a community group who eventually capped the exposed mineralized rock and restored the health of the river."

Roger's wife, Liz, asked, "So, a mining company can create a big mess and people like you and Dan come in and clean it up for them so they can go out and do it again elsewhere? Regardless of the goodness of your intentions, aren't you just helping them destroy the earth?"

"I bet many of you have been, or are, tree planters?" Dan replied. "Isn't that like promoting clear-cutting by helping the forestry companies achieve regen levels, so then they can mow down the next swath?"

"Yeah, but trees grow back in our lifetime. You can rehab an open pit with shrubs and hardy plants but I think it's still putting lipstick on a pig."

"Choose your evil, I guess," Dan responded. "Your photovoltaic panels, electric cars, cell phones, home computers, pots and pans—hardly a moment goes by without any of us using non-renewable minerals. Some even come with an incredible social and environmental cost, like the rare earth metals produced in some developing countries. Don't imagine for a moment I'd work for operations like that. But I don't want to be a hypocrite, so I do the best I can. Someone has to do it. And that's me."

He spoke with such sincerity, no one had a reply.

"Okay, moving on. Brookfield has studies that suggest Pyrite Island, and this site in particular, may have deposits that would be well worth excavating. Here are the documents outlining a possible course of action *if* I find what the senior geologists think *may* be present."

Garba sat forward in her deck chair and asked, "But Derek and his wife have title to the one hundred and fifty acres here, don't they have the final word?"

"Yes, they have the surface rights, but unfortunately not what may be below ground. Surface rights are just that—the titles for the timber and other chattels on top of the bedrock."

"What does this history lesson have to do with us here today at Linton's Beach? Just so you know, my name is Garba Bean, and I'm sort of an unofficial spokesperson for those of us on the island."

"Nice to meet you, Garba. Well, besides the main land grant, there were some offshore areas included as well. Probably for possible subsurface potential. Lines drawn on a map marking off areas here and there, based on local names such as Pyrite Island and visual indicators of minerals."

"Such as?"

"Outcroppings of ore-bearing rock, staining, seeps and leachates, even some plants. All of which we can verify with geophones and listening to the echoes from controlled detonations."

"So, after all these big words, you mean you intend to set off explosions around the cove to peek into the rocky heart of our island? And if you find what you suspect is here, what next?"

"Well, the company would move in a drilling crew and expand the exploration to neighbouring properties with similar characteristics. But that is another department and I'm not involved in that. They'll send a rep to meet with you before anything like that happens. Someone with more seniority and heft."

"And bags of money, I suppose?"

Dan nodded. "Always money."

Garba said, "Here, we're trying to get away from that. We rely on barter, co-operation, a free store next to the post office. That kinda stuff."

After a moment, Dan handed her the papers.

"Have a good look at this. Tomorrow I'm going to cruise around, if that's okay. Garba, when you are through with reading that stack of information, maybe a public meeting might be appropriate."

"Yeah, but it may not be comfortable for you." She knew how issues like this tore across the island, getting distorted like in the child's game where a phrase is passed from one to another, the final words rarely resembling the original.

"Goes with the job, but thanks for the warning." His smile never wavered. "How about we meet up tomorrow, in case you have any questions?"

"Sure. I'll give you a call, what's your number?"

"No cell phone for me, just a VHF radio on the boat and a sat phone for emergencies. I like to travel incognito."

"Okay, how about we just meet down by the wharf around nine. We can grab a coffee."

Derek walked Dan back down to the beach, where his boat was bobbing in the small waves. Purple seaweed swirled amid fat oysters in the shallows.

"It's a funny business, mineral exploration and mining, Derek. Trading pain for a few for the gain of many. Or is it the other way around. Sometimes I wonder." He bent down to pick up a flat rock from the shore, skipped it twice on the wavy surface.

"I ran into a friend recently," Derek said, his hands in his pockets, "another UBC grad. Forestry. Said he'd just quit his job. Laying out cutblocks in first growth up-coast. Got to be he couldn't sleep at night. Near the end, he started reducing the timber volumes and increasing the impediments to road access. He knew he'd get caught sooner or later, so he walked away from it all. Brave man."

In a low voice, Dan asked, "You suggesting I fudge my ore samples if I find something of interest to Brookfield? Downgrade the results?"

Derek shrugged. "Been done many times before. Usually, the other way around. Salting the cores with higher-grade ore to attract development investment." But he shook his head, adding, "No, I am aware of and have myself always adhered to professional ethics. Perhaps you'd allow me to look at the seismic data before you release the findings to Brookfield? I'm not questioning your work, Dan; I just want to stay ahead of the... inevitable uproar."

"Sure, that sounds okay." He turned and reached out his hand. "And on that note, my friend, I think I'll turn in. Busy day tomorrow. I suspect I will have company."

Mid-shake, Derek added, "You're welcome to stay at the house."

"Thanks, but I really like being rocked by the waves. Don't have any trouble getting to sleep."

He headed toward the boat, then looked back over his shoulder at Derek.

"And, if there is the 'uproar' you mentioned, might be best if we aren't seen as too chummy."

Garba was up all night poring over the maps, the technical data and the immensity of the proposed project. Map symbols superimposed over much of Linton's Beach and nearby lands. Outlines of a yawning pit, haul roads, crushing mill, conveyors and loading dock. She shook her head in disbelief.

The next morning, Dan took his boat around to the government wharf and met Garba for coffee.

After they settled into their seats at Red Tide Seafood Ltd., Garba spoke bluntly. "Dan, while I truly appreciate you providing me with this proposal, I am astounded you have the audacity to be part of such an intrusion. The scope of disturbance will be actively resisted, I can assure you."

"Nothing will happen out of sequence. Brookfield will not progress until my exploration determines any value. Can I ask that you keep this to yourself for now?"

"Okay, but what's in it for you? Fame and glory? Cash?"

"Who'd you rather have? A wage earner on their payroll or me, a vagabond consultant living on a boat, poking around with a light footprint? A hundred years ago, I'd probably be called a prospector—but instead of a donkey and pickaxe, I have a motorboat and a computer."

"I'd rather you just went away, Dan."

"Brookfield is aware of Pyrite Island, like it or not. As I said, they won't make a move unless my preliminary data shows promise. Which it may or... just may not."

He fell silent, looking past her, to the dock, to his boat.

She gave a reluctant but conditional nod.

"Can you find me a couple of strong workers to pack my supplies along the transects? Not going to use explosives for this part. There's a new technique with propane, like the cannons in the vineyards in the Okanagan. For shallow depths, a lot less noise and surface disturbance for the geophones to record."

"Good. I'll call the Nichepkos. They have a couple of skookum sons, Carl and Fuzz, who work now and then at the limestone quarry over on Turtle Island. They like motorcycles and explosions. A bit rough around the edges, but good workers and honest. Island born and raised."

While the boys were being summoned, Dan returned to an anchorage a couple bays down from Linton's Beach and set out his gear on the shore. After taking a few compass bearings, he booted up his iPad and located some GIS reference points for his survey. He headed out in a straight line, hanging pink flagging ribbon at intervals, purposefully putting distance between him and the new old house at the cove.

Soon, he heard hooting and crashing through the bush. The Nichepko boys appeared, clearly in their late teens and able-bodied for the work, but with bright smiles and a happy recklessness in their eyes that reminded Dan of puppies. The two brothers greeted him with handshakes and an eager inquiry.

"We're here to help you blow holes in the ground, right?"

"Well, yes. Did Garba tell you why?"

"Yup, she said you were looking for gold nuggets, bars of silver, and diamonds just under the surface, ready to pluck up. She had to use the island party line, though," Fuzz said.

"Is that a good thing?"

"Suppose it depends on who was eavesdropping. Some people listen in for entertainment, others as self-appointed vigilantes. If you haven't heard a new rumour before noon, start one."

Dan nodded and showed them the equipment. A propane bottle, a small, motorized rock drill, several pipes and fittings, and heavy metal plates with long wires connecting to his iPad.

"What we're going to do is drill a few holes into the ground a measured distance apart, fill them with propane, drop in a piezo igniter like you'd use for a barbeque, clamp a lid on it, hook it up to my computer and set it off. The vibration echo shows a profile of the underground strata. Then, with my brilliant intelligence and vast experience, I can make an educated blind guess as to what lies below the shrubbery."

When he mentioned the explosion, both boys got wide-eyed.

The procedure went textbook. The resulting bangs were unimpressive to the helpers, but the graph showed a series of squiggles, which Dan examined slowly. Each time they retrieved the wire and scraped a bit of loose rock and moss over the shot hole, leaving barely a scuff in the ground.

The rest of the day was the same, though Carl and Fuzz pleaded with Dan to load more gas to make a spectacular display.

Dan politely refused. "Not here, not now."

Undismayed, they pressed him hopefully. "Okay. Where? When?"

"Ten more. Are we on your family's land yet? Anybody at home?"

They looked around to locate themselves. Rocky knob, a couple of shaggy feral sheep watching and placidly chewing, firs with thick bark like fissured concrete, flaky tangerine orange arbutus, and Oregon grape with skeins of dusky purple berries.

"Yeah. We used to have a treehouse up in that tree. No one's home. Dad's fishing, Mom is at a tai chi class at the community hall and our sister is at high school over there." Carl pointed across the Strait. "The blue rinse capital of the Island. Traffic jams of golf carts and electric scooters."

Motivated by the unspoken promise, the brothers worked twice as fast to finish the shots. More bangs, more squiggles, then packing the equipment out to the Nichepkos' rutted road. Dan sensed someone shadowing them in the nearby forest, but no one else did.

They walked into the farmyard clearing, dropped their loads. Fuzz went into the house and brought back three stubby bottles of cold homemade beer.

Dan slaked his thirst then asked the brothers, "Newton said, 'For every action there is an equal and opposite reaction.' Do you know what he meant?"

The boys shook their heads. "Does it go boom?" asked Carl.

Dan looked around behind the barn and came out with a cracked twenty-litre bucket. He turned it upside down, slid an igniter under it, packed mud around the rim and stuck the propane nozzle inside.

"Go find a safe place to watch from," he said, opening the propane for a longer period than usual to load the gas. Then he turned it off and joined the boys behind a tree. With a flip of a switch the piezo sparked and with a huge boom, the bucket was launched in pieces. Carl let out a whoop as Fuzz yelled, "Yeah!" Dan watched the screen as the lines danced.

"Huh, that's odd. Feel that?" He looked at the ground.

"Yeah, it's still wiggling," Fuzz replied. "Now it's stopped."

Dan pointed to the iPad and hit a few keys to overlay all the previous shots. A jagged peak soared far above them.

"Odd. Shouldn't have been that much disturbance, even with the bigger charge."

Carl went into the house for another round of beer and came running back out.

"Geez, guys! Come and see this."

Dan and Fuzz dashed into the back door and looked at the kitchen. Several cabinet doors were flung open and some broken dishes were scattered on the floor.

"Did we do that?"

Dan scratched his head and shrugged.

"Let's clean it up and keep it between us for now. At least until I get another opinion, okay?"

"Sure, no problem," Fuzz said. "Wouldn't know how to explain it if I tried."

That evening, after having supper with Derek and Linda, Dan tried to casually ask about the spike from the geophones.

"Everything is going well on the preliminary surface measurements. One or two things you might find amusing or at least of interest. At times I felt like I was being watched but no one came and talked to me or asked what we were doing. The shots were small enough that no fly rock was produced." He paused and looked at Linda.

"The other item is kinda technical; I need to discuss it with the venerable expert."

"Sure, I'll leave you to your rock talk. Heaven knows I've had my fill of it over the years," she added with a laugh. "I'll take my evening stroll."

Derek watched her go and turned to Dan with a raised eyebrow. Opening his iPad, Dan showed him the readings from the day and explained the last shot.

"Did it mainly to amuse the boys."

Derek studied the abnormality, comparing it to the previous readings. He looked at the time display of the shot.

"At 1600 hours... Four in the afternoon? Maybe it's an ingrained habit from an old field rock hound, but I remember feeling a rumble sometime around then. I first thought it was Roger delivering a load of drain rock for the septic field, but there was no truck. No jet or helicopter from the Comox air base. Got any idea if there is some link with your last overloaded shot?"

"No. Was hoping you would."

Derek stood up and went to his cluttered desk, returning with a map.

"I have one far-fetched idea, but it's one that is occurring elsewhere so drawing parallel conclusions isn't too difficult. This is a map of tectonic plates in the Strait of Georgia. The Juan de Fuca oceanic plate, on which perches Vancouver Island, is being pushed under, subducted, by the North American plate. As you know, this compression causes three types of earthquakes in the basin: crustal, deeper subduction, and very large deeper shakes on the plate boundaries."

"And my strongest shot may've triggered a shallow release? Like those caused by fracking on the prairies? But it was a tiny pop compared to that deep drilling and pressurized injection of mud and chemicals."

Derek looked out the window toward the cove as if expecting the answer to bubble to the surface. He bent over the map, pulled Dan's iPad over and began hammering at it, searching various websites before he found what he was looking for.

"Here, look at this." He jabbed a finger at the screen. "It's an enlargement of the plate's eastern rift. Not too far offshore here. And only two or three kilometres deep."

He scrolled down to check some of the footnotes.

"Okay, there has been more detailed sonar and bathyscaphic surveying. There appears to be extensive recent intrusions of heavily mineralized magma."

"Hot rock?"

"Yeah, but the stratum is thin, vertical and slippery between the plates."

"You suggesting it's unstable and liable to be set off by the next step of large-scale drilling for core sampling? Earthquakes and displacement. Which brings up the possibility of a…"

"Tsunami in a shallow basin?"

For the next week, Dan and the brothers continued to make soundings on the west side of Pirate Island, mainly on the Martin and Nichepko properties. Dan clenched his teeth with each shallow shot and resisted the pleading of the boys to destroy something, like one of the dusty and moss-covered vehicles slowly oxidizing beneath the rampant Scotch broom. With each detonation Dan waited for an unusual rumble, but there was none.

Satisfied, he said, "Well, that's a wrap guys. Thank you for your help this week."

"No problem," said Carl. "Any interest in seeing the rest of the island? We could show you around."

"Sure, why not." He gathered up his gear and hopped into an old truck the boys managed to start. It had no windshield, one door was duct-taped shut and the licence plate was seven years expired.

"The cops only come over once or twice a year and everyone knows quickly from the telephone tree. Like any warning system, fire or earthquake," Carl explained. But his choice of words caused Dan to twitch.

He squinted at a small figure on the side of the road ahead.

"Looks like a hitchhiker. I'll hop in the back if you want to pick him up," Dan offered.

"No need. That's Johnny O. He's a professional hermit. He's headed down to the store for his weekly supply run. His pack board is empty so he won't need a ride. Coming back loaded with cans and kerosene, he may suffer and take a lift. But now, watch him."

As predicted, when Johnny O. turned to see the truck approaching, a look of panic twisted his face and he dove, nearly headfirst, into the thicket of salmonberry and thrashed into hiding, motionless until they passed.

"Sometimes we stop and see how long he'll stay in the brush without twitching. He's like a spotted fawn. People say he's some sort of remittance man."

"What is that?"

"Used to be a guy from England who was sent to the 'colonies' to spare the upper-class family embarrassment," Carl explained, "perhaps escape a vengeful father or irate husband. Living on family money, until it runs out. Nowadays, we'd probably call them 'trustafarians.' We got a few of those."

"But some of them fit right in," Fuzz added, "and really contribute to the good of everyone. Like a guy down at Millie's Lagoon—raised a bunch of money from his connections in Victoria to buy an ambulance. Decertified but good enough for us, considering what we had before. Nothing."

The road curved around and over arid knolls of rock tufted with several shades and textures of moss, stubborn twisted oaks and bonsai pines. What amazed Dan were the verdant hollows cupped between the basalt hummocks. Nearly every one was encircled by a deer fence protecting lush gardens and orchards around buildings of peculiar design and construction.

Noticing Dan's interest in these oases and the homes they surrounded, Carl said proudly, "If you're curious about Pirate Island's rad buildings, we can take you to one that's really cool: our community hall."

A few minutes later, they stopped in a cloud of dust facing what Dan initially thought was an enormous pile of driftwood and logs. He recalled in one of his undergrad paleozoology courses the mention of a giant beaver the size of a bear in the Pleistocene, which may've built lodges of this scale.

They slid across the threadbare seat and out the only functional door and stood looking at the building. Windows and doors were now visible through the settling dust. Inside, Dan stood open-mouthed, looking at the soaring beams and interwoven purlins and rafters, no two alike, but neither did they look happenstance. The open area was cathedralic. Geodesic dome, mammoth tipi, yurt—or elements of all of them.

"Amazing. All handcrafted, too, I imagine."

"Yup," said Fuzz. "When they started building the hall we had a scavenger hunt for the most unusual driftwood on the island. Animal forms, fantasy creatures, were used for beams, trusses and rafters."

"Not as fragile as you might think either," added Carl. "Stood up to several gales. And in an earthquake, it'd groan and wobble, but remain standing."

Dan looked at the lofty ceiling and wondered why the boys had so casually mentioned earthquakes twice today. The blast must still be on their minds, he figured. He hoped they stuck to their word and kept quiet about it. A small group sat around a table for a painting class led by a woman with streaked pink hair. They turned to see Dan and the boys. Fuzz waved at one of them.

"Our mom," he explained. "Lots of groups meet here, especially in the winter, when cabin fever hits us after weeks of grey. We'd be playing volleyball next to the capoeira practice, with a string band howling in the corner. Into the evening, or until the generator ran dry."

There was a murmur and a second glance, then the artists returned to their creative work. The trio continued the island tour, ending back at the wharf and store. *Serendipity* bumped softly against the black timbers. The boys stepped aboard as Dan pointed out the few amenities.

"Wow, so you live on the boat and cruise around doing this geology stuff? I'd like to do that. Sounds like a perfect world," Carl exclaimed.

"Can be. Though there are times when it's not. Storms, rain, miserable bosses, confrontations, nasty tides. Four years of university and a curious mind set you up. And a boat, of course."

Carl ran his hand over the steering wheel. "I might just look into that."

As the brothers made to leave, Dan said, "Thanks for the tour, and for the help with the field work." The boys watched as he opened a drawer and peeled off a few fifties and handed them over. "Probably see you at the public meeting Garba is arranging?"

"Wouldn't miss it for anything. Good luck."

That evening, Dan sat on his boat sampling a bit of the island's best. Above him the tiki lights from the pub blinked and voices and music drifted down to him. But he did not feel like being social. After working over his notes—and still puzzled about the initial anomaly and a few less noticeable ones—he heard footsteps coming down the wharf ramp.

"Permission to come aboard, captain?" asked Garba.

"Have your passport ready for inspection."

He showed her the accommodations: propane stove, built-in kitchen with small sink, set of drawers and closet, fold-down table seating two, and a pile of sleeping bags on a V-berth under the front deck.

"All I need."

"Quite cozy, but..." As was her habit, she came right to the point. "I've scheduled a CRAP public meeting for tomorrow night at the community hall. I assume you are available?"

"Wouldn't miss it for anything."

"I'll attempt to maintain some semblance of order, but word has spread that you are surveying for mining potential. Like I said, it may get a bit toasty for you. Okay with that?"

"No torches, rope and pitchforks, I hope. Yeah, I'm just going to present some clarification on the process."

She looked seriously at Dan.

"How can you do this for a living? Coming to a community and turning it inside out? Then sailing off into the sunset leaving smoking desolation behind you?"

"I just do the initial..."

"Yeah, I get that. Just following orders. Heard that many times in nasty situations."

"Information is a powerful tool, Garba. Substance and timing are everything." He stared at her and waited. "And friends may be where you least expect them."

She stood up, found her balance and stepped onto the dock. "See you at the meeting. I'll be there early."

And so was Dan. Since his first visit with the brothers, he had learned that the community hall was located at the crossroads of the two main potholed gravel roads bisecting the island. Like many landmarks, the intersection was known for previous homesteaders and notable events: the old O'Brien farm, the Feisty House (the couple who argued continually through their many years together), and the corner where Speedy Jack hit a free-range cow with his motorbike. As he walked up the road across from the hall he saw the community mailbox, faded green and rusty. Few operable padlocks hung from the hasps; most boxes were open and held local notices, plants, envelopes without stamps for island delivery.

Again Dan felt a sense of wonder as he entered the superbly constructed dome. It seemed that the majority of the islanders were early as well. This time the hall was filled with people, milling around rows of chairs. Garba had enlarged several maps and diagrams relating to the project and posted them along the walls. Intense discussions, fingers tracing property lines, all subsided when he entered with his small handful of papers. He took a deep breath, smiled, and joined Garba at the head table. He handed her his memory stick of the same charts and more photos. She squeezed an old-fashioned bicycle horn and asked everyone to take a seat. Dan noticed a few familiar faces: the Nichepko family, Derek and Linda and their friends, Garba's sisters, and Ted and Monica, the store owners.

"I'm sure everyone has some questions, but let's try to keep it open and respectful. I will summarize what I know from the documents Dan provided, then turn it over to him. In essence, Brookfield Mineral Enterprises wants to develop the subterranean ores found under roughly the entire southwest corner of our island. They have applied to the province for the necessary permits." She traced the area on one of the displayed maps and briefly spoke to the extent of the work proposed. "The project is staggering in its scale and presumptions."

A rumble like the one at the Nichepkos' rose from the attendees. A few hands went up.

"Please save your questions until Dan has finished his presentation. I am starting a speakers list. Everyone will get their opportunity. But first, let Dan give an overview."

He stood up and walked across to the charts, maps and diagrams that outlined the proposal steps, the land involved and the legal requirements of subsurface and surface rights. It took ten minutes, as the audience fidgeted and squirmed, and then Dan turned things back over to Garba.

Garba looked at her clipboard for the first questioner. As expected, it was Bosko.

"Who's gonna benefit from this mine?"

"From the proposal, they say the usual," said Dan. "Jobs, possible electricity, and royalties to the affected landowners."

"Royalties? Like payments?"

"Compensation for the landowners for access to the projected ore body." He paused and explained. "They refer to removing the 'overburden,' which is everything on top of the mineral strata."

There was a long, heavy silence. Liz raised her hand and asked in a shaky voice, "Everything? Trees, dirt, buildings, homes, ponds? And this so-called overburden, the living, breathing flesh of the island, where's it gonna go?"

"They don't mention that. It will be part of the yet-to-come remediation plan." Dan glanced at Derek quickly. He gave a slight shake of his head but did not respond.

At this, several people got up and walked out, thinking they'd heard enough.

Garba called to them, "Wait, we need to hear all the facts and make plans for action."

A few returned to their seats, but several had shot scathing looks at Dan and Derek before leaving.

"Your turn still, Dan. Convince us."

"Okay. This is the area where Brookfield wanted my initial survey. Each dot represents a shot hole and seismic echo recorded by a geophone and my computer. Here's what it looks like."

He showed a graph with a sawtooth line, regular in height and frequency except for one place where the flat line erupted in a set of squiggles. No one asked about it. Not yet.

"This shows the level of ore-bearing formations. Doesn't say what kind it might contain. A larger drill and more explosive detonations would determine that. But that would come only after my data is analyzed and other factors addressed. Then and only then would they proceed."

"Well, then, what did this preliminary data tell you, and them?" asked Ted. "If you struck gold, I'd better get in a big order of beer." A polite but small chortle attempted to reduce the tension but failed.

"I can't tell you that. It's the intellectual property of Brookfield at this time, whether it's another Klondike or a dry hole."

A senior in overalls stood up. "My name is Darrel Jorgeson. Can you go back to the one showing all the lines around here? I used to be a salmon troller and depended on charts to avoid rocks and shallows, so this kinda map interests me."

"Will do," said Dan, returning to that chart. "These lines represent the approximate boundaries of the tectonic plates, which I am sure you have all heard of. Ever jostling each other, these slabs of the earth's crust float on a lake of liquid roiling rock, magma, of unimaginable heat and pressure. The term 'Ring of Fire' says it quite well. This is where the ancient meets the present. Volcanos, geysers, hot springs and grinding geologic arm-wrestling occurs. In 1946, Mount Washington buckled and moved nearly a metre on a diagonal plane. How many million tons of basalt and granite was in that shrug? Epicentre was under Forbidden Plateau. There is a surface offset easily visible in the Cruikshank Canyon.

"The ocean floor over at Deep Bay dropped one and a half metres. And it caused a considerable landslide on the side of Mount Colonel Foster, damming the Elk River and creating a lake."

"So that red line on that map is a crack in the crust where this devil's coffee pot is bubbling?" asked Darrel. "And there's a piece of a tectonic plate blocking it?"

"It's between a chip and a fragment; squeezed like a watermelon seed between the North American Continental Plate and the Pacific Plate. It's so small, previous surveys have either failed to identify it or it's only recently been detected and not researched fully.

"So, yes, the red line is an intrusion of highly mineralized magma between these chips."

"Dangerous?"

"Probably not any more than fishing in a gale on the Queen Charlotte Strait." Another laugh languished.

Johnny O., who Dan recognized from the roadside, was next. Living alone with his dog Lizzie and hiding when anyone unexpected came to his cabin, he was out of the practice of conversation, but today he was fairly bursting to speak.

"Okay, forget about all your technical words and numbers and backtrack a bit so's I can figure out how all this pimple of God's butt came to be, 'cause I smell a rat... If someone with connections to the mining industry gets wind of this bonanza under Pirate Island, so he goes and uses this insider information to buy up the land on top of it, but not wanting to set off any premature alarms, he poses as another city refugee looking for a holiday spot on the ocean, and then another buddy just happens to show up with his electric eyes to see through rock and finds the gold or whatever and tells the big company, then fucks off to the next job leaving the other guy sitting pretty with his future well guaranteed by the royalty payments. Nice work, eh?" All of it spewed forth in one breath, Johnny O. deflated back onto his chair with a smug grin on his face. No one said a word. Garba eyed Derek, who was red-faced and tight-lipped. Linda reached across and laid her hand on his knee. Garba heard Dan take a deep inhale but before he could respond, she took the floor.

"Well, that's the most I ever heard you utter in a single sentence. World premiere. Anyone else you want to implicate in your insider conspiracy theory?"

Johnny O. leapt to his feet like a jack-in-the-box. "Yeah, Garba. You."

She sat stunned for a moment. "Would you like to tell us how you came to this opinion?"

"Nope. Well, maybe Daddy's pockets are running low."

Garba gave him a withering look. "Just because I step up and take charge is no reason to make this personal. This is an information meeting, not a debate on anyone's personal ethics." She turned to the rest of the residents. "Does anyone have any questions about geology, drilling or government regulations?"

"Question for Dan," Ted said. "That fissure you've redlined; how big is it?"

"About two kilometres long and fifty to sixty metres wide. Don't know how deep."

"Okay, then. If this chip was to be, say, dislodged by a more aggressive drilling operation—which is what you say would be the next procedure, if your data proves out—and it were to slip or release the compression, what would happen here on the island?"

"This is only my semi-educated guess, but, depending on the rapidity, depth and size of the displaced fragment, a subduction slip could create a considerable surface wave. The Strait's a rather narrow and shallow basin, which might amplify the..."

"A tsunami?" Ted interrupted.

Dan looked at Derek who gave a slight shrug. "Yes. The 1946 shake hit nearby Turtle Island with two waves that were two to three metres high. It was a 7.5 on the Richter scale. Yes, there was some damage to the docks."

"I remember that," said the retired fisherman. "I was just a kid, sitting on my bunk putting on my boots. Just thought it was a wake, but it kept running up and down the channel for a spell."

The gathering erupted in a dozen conversations. Taken aback by Johnny O.'s insinuations, Derek and Linda left the hall amidst the pandemonium. A knot of people had gathered in front of Dan and Garba when Derek shoved his way back through them.

"Who the hell wrecked my truck? Bastards. We haven't been anything but good neighbours to all of you."

Dan and Garba followed him outside and stood staring at his truck.

In bright red paint were the words "Traitor" and "Go Home."

Linda sat in the truck staring at Garba, eyes wide in disbelief, or perhaps just disappointment. Derek joined her, ground the gears into reverse and fishtailed off in a spray of gravel.

Dan looked at the crowd, but no one would meet his eyes.

He turned to Garba. "I gotta go. Can you give me a ride back to the wharf? If my boat is damaged too..." Dan gathered his papers, then they hopped into her old Toyota wagon, which was held together by layers of bumper stickers for past causes, and followed the dust cloud down the road.

As Garba drove, Dan replayed the meeting in his mind. "What did that obnoxious twerp mean about Daddy's pockets?"

"A few people here have off-island income from pensions, previous land sales, investments or family money. Others struggle with making enough income to live on. Money from unemployment insurance, fishing, tree planting, growing pot, making arts and crafts soon runs out. Then they get angry at those they consider unfairly subsidized."

"And the runt considers you one of the nouveau riche?"

"I guess so. When I turned twenty-one, I was given some shares that have increased in value over the years, from a family company. Ironically enough, the growth was supported, in a small part, by the purchases of outdoor clothing by the hiking and outdoor folks.

"Even you, perhaps. You've heard of L.L. Bean?"

Dan flipped his hat over and there was the familiar logo, faded by wear but still legible.

"Never put it together, Garba. That company, you and your sisters' last name. Everyone gets suspicious of corporate connections. But the truth is a lot of people support corporations like Brookfield and don't even know it: pension funds for teachers, provincial employees, journalists. No one is immune to the web. Maybe not even Johnny O."

"And you, Dan? Any filthy lucre on your hands?"

"No, not that I am aware of. The pleasure and perils of the self-unemployed. Free to starve," he joked.

They pulled onto the wharf, where the *Serendipity* was moored, and climbed out of the car to check the boat for damage. No sign of vandalism, no lines cut or painted profanities. High slack tide. Not a ripple disturbed the night-dark water. A few reflections were perfect mirror images: his boat, the stubby ferry, lights from the store.

Dan thanked Garba for the ride. He thought about asking her aboard for a nightcap, but decided the evening's events had left them both worn thin.

"I'll drop by to see you tomorrow morning," she said. "We should go talk to Derek and Linda, see what we can do to calm everyone down."

"That's probably a good first step," Dan said, then added, with emphasis, "Looking forward to it."

After momentary surprise, Garba said, "Me too." She gave Dan a hug goodbye, along with a not-so-quick kiss on the cheek, then got back into her Toyota. After backing off the wharf, she turned the car around and spun up the hill.

In the new old house, Derek sat quietly with Linda at his desk, only a small lamp lit.

"We can't let the action of a couple of hotheads destroy us, Derek. This place is something you have dreamed about for years. You made it happen, no one else could have put all the pieces together: finding the land, the heritage house, our plans for the future. We have everything invested in this. I'm not giving up and neither are you."

"Fight or flight, then?"

"No, those are not our only choices. Strength, truth, high ground."

He got up and went to the window. Starlight illuminated the cove. After a minute's contemplation, he turned back to his desk.

"Thank you for that reminder," he said, walking over and giving her a kiss. "Go to bed, my love. I have work to do. More pieces to put together."

As Linda headed upstairs, he opened a small metal filing cabinet and pulled out several thick folders and binders. After sorting through them, he booted up his desktop and began writing.

The next morning, Linda descended the creaky old stairs and looked into Derek's office. As expected, he lay with his head on his crossed forearms on a stack of papers. Entering the kitchen, she lit the propane stove and made coffee. The scent drifted through the early light, eliciting a groan from the next room.

"Here, you look like you might need this. Worked all night? Satisfied?"

Derek reached for the hot cup with gratitude. "Yeah, but it's not easy."

"Revenge? Justice? Reconciliation?"

"Maybe a bit of all those. Not much of the first, though."

He pointed to three big envelopes. "Let people make up their own minds."

He called Fuzz Nichepko and asked him to drop off an envelope to Garba at her desk in the community hall. "Anonymously, for now," he added, and thanked the boy. He slipped another into a larger envelope and addressed it to a courier service in the city to be forwarded. The last package he addressed to the business services desk at the post office, enclosing a one-page cover sheet for faxing it all to the national broadcaster. He'd drop both off at the ferry.

He disliked the secrecy but cleared his mind by thinking of it as "gardening": planting seeds in fertile ground and letting them grow as they might.

All three reached their intended audiences simultaneously, as he had hoped.

The mayor of the retirement mecca on the big island to the west opened the envelope, scanned the first page and gasped. He hurriedly called his staff planner and public works supervisor. He was fairly sputtering when they rushed into his office.

"Holy cow, look at this." He shoved a paper across his desk.

Newly Discovered Tectonic Faultline

From recent local geologic explorations, a crack in the earth's crust has been discovered nearby. When, not if, it releases, a wave and tremor may create a one-to-two-metre tsunami impacting the east coast of the island, specifically the area of Coronado Shores Estates, High Tide Casino and the civic marina. If it matches the intensity and scope of the 1946 earthquake, subsidence and displacement of lowlands and unstable cliffs may also result.

See enclosed references for more information.

"Who sent this?" asked the works boss.

"Dunno. Shirley said it was delivered this morning by courier. There's no name on it, but the reports are all attributed to scientists, not eco-freaks. Published public domain studies from the past five years."

He slid the envelope across his desk. "Read this and get back to me soon. If this gets out..."

His secretary poked her nose into his office.

"Uh, Mark Sorenson from the *Island Times* is on the phone. Wants to talk to you about this earthquake tsunami story."

She left to answer her phone and quickly returned.

"Two more calls, one from a newspaper in the city and another from the owners of the casino."

"Oh, crap. Who else?"

His own cell phone rang and he looked at it like it was a poisonous snake.

Garba sat in the community hall's office, staring at the pages of reports. Dan had claimed he had no knowledge of the package or the identity of the sender. He had mailed his own findings to Brookfield a day earlier but did not mention the presence of the fault, only the interpretations of his preliminary low-level seismic sampling, omitting the single anomaly and the broken dishes at the Nichepkos'.

Her cell phone warbled and she too was facing a barrage of questions, first from an acquaintance who wrote for an environmental weekly. The news spread, and with the creative licence of journalists following hot leads, the story grew like wildfire.

At Coronado Shores Estates it was soon on everyone's lips: In the multi-million-dollar homes, under the thatched roofs of the beach palapas and around the softly lit gaming tables of the High Tide Casino, people stood at the seaward windows, listening for a rumble and looking for a bubble or warning ripple. Tanned yachtsmen in crisp white shorts and polo shirts climbed onto the tops of their yachts and scanned the ocean beyond the breakwater. They looked for the unnatural swell that would pummel their fibreglass hulls against the jagged granite rocks, then roil up onto the golf course, eroding the immaculate greens and curvaceous fairways. The second wave might even undermine the sandy soils supporting the gambling halls and the four-storey condos. Oceanfront views suddenly became a liability rather than an asset.

The civic engineer reported back to the mayor.

"A company called Brookfield Mineral Enterprises has been taking out subsurface licences and may begin large-scale sample drilling on Pyrite and Turtle Islands. Legal works."

"Get hold of their CEO. Tell them it's urgent."

The evening news led with the story of how a luxury beach community might be in imminent danger from a possible catastrophic tsunami from a shallow undersea disturbance, possibly caused by seismic blasting and drilling. There was no mention of the company involved and enough weasel words like "perhaps," "possibly" and "maybe" to pass the scrutiny of the editors and legal advisors.

A camera crew arrived at city hall and interviewed a perspiring mayor, then went into the casino to get some citizen reaction. They were promptly escorted back outside by security personnel, adding to the tension.

Derek and Linda watched the drama unfold on their computer screen. Late in the coverage, a flustered spokesman for Brookfield claimed innocence. He had only just received a preliminary report from their field geologist on Pyrite Island. Now the attention turned there with force.

"Probably wouldn't get five minutes on the late news if it was just us, but since it affects the well-off retirees over there, not just a scraggly bunch of old hippies, it's going to be front page all week," Garba observed, sitting in the café talking to Dan and watching the foot passengers come and go off the ferry. A number of them were clearly reporters with no idea where they were going, just milling around near the wharf, hoping to stumble onto the story. It had been three days since the arrival of the anonymous packages and the media storm they unleashed.

Garba's phone kept beeping.

"Poor little thing. Overworked recently." She looked at the screen. "Oh, this could be interesting. It's Brookfield. Why would they have my number?"

"I suspect yours is the only number anyone has for Pyrite Island."

Garba answered the call, paused to listen, then said, "Yes, I can contact him. Oh, he just came in. I'll pass the phone over. Mr. Lawrence, call for you on line one." She suppressed a giggle.

He took it and listened quietly.

"Okay, if you think that is the proper response. Goodbye."

"Well?"

"I'm fired. And the HR woman said they would ensure I will never ever get another contract from them or their affiliates. They are questioning my results from the seismic testing, too, and think I was the one who sent the info to the media. I talked to them just yesterday and explained I was as much in the dark as anyone. But I guess they needed a scapegoat."

"Jeez, Dan. Hope I wasn't part of the reason. What're you going to do now? I mean, can they blackball you from your career? Forever?"

"It's a small world, mineral exploration. Not a whole lot of new faces and most of them are going north to the tar sands projects. Maybe this is a blessing in disguise, Garba. I've been getting tired of it anyways. Not what I want to look back on."

"What is, then?"

Dan stared across the bay toward the mountains in the west. "I was my happiest on my own when I was a summer student, scratching around in likely gravel with pan and sluice, looking for gold in my off-times." He turned back to Garba and ran his hand through his hair. "Not that I can rewind the years that easily," he added with a dramatic sigh.

"Garba, I've been in some incredible country with no one looking over my shoulder except for an occasional bear, more curious than threatening. No bureaucrats, no politicians, no company bosses. Wild country. Makes your Pirate Island look suburban." The immediacy in his voice evoked a realm of wilderness just out there, waiting for his return. "What about you? I suppose living the alt community lifestyle here is your idea of paradise, but have you ever wondered what else is out there?"

Garba thought for a minute and traced circles on the table with her coffee cup spills.

"Been doing this island life for more than twenty years, Dan. Yeah, I think it is a good way to live. But sometimes it gets both too intense and too predictable, even for me. Grow your own toothpaste. Dance naked under the solstice moon.

"Sometimes it seems like I have to conform to the expectations of the nonconformists; and sometimes the points don't make sense. Like, if you're for saving the transient orcas, you'd be against the cull of harbour seals, even though they are eating all the Chinook salmon, the orcas' main food.

"At the public meeting, I actually envied crazy Johnny O. for at least speaking his own mind, regardless of what everyone might have thought. Or thought but didn't have the nerve to admit. One of these days, I want to put up a Conservative election sign on my fence, just to rattle the cage a bit."

"Is this the proclaimed Queen of CRAP speaking?" he joked.

"Yeah, I know," Garba said. "Anyway, maybe going off with a donkey, gold pan, pick and shovel looking for riches isn't so unbelievable—maybe it's even downright sensible."

She then asked a question that had been on her mind. "That ring on your finger, what does it mean?"

He held up his hand and the ring caught the light.

"It's gold. From a river near Dease Lake. The little flakes and dust were purified in the metallurgy lab at UBC, then cast in the sculpture studio. It's just a ring to remind me that there are different kinds of value, different sorts of desires."

He paused, then added, "It might mean more to someone someday, in another time." He absently slipped it off and rolled it around on the table. "End of their rainbow." Then he replaced it on his finger.

Over the next week, the media scrum beleaguered Brookfield from all sectors: tourism, real estate, oyster farms, fishermen, boat owners and environmental organizations. Even schoolchildren drew pictures of giant waves incongruously flaming with hot magma. The company soon announced the preliminary exploration data did not depict adequate minerals for further work and they withdrew their applications. Their parting shot, however, did make reference to all the detractors conveniently overlooking their own use of metal produced by mining. As if that said it all.

Early winter storms began visiting Pirate Island. Winds rolled up the Strait. Days of drizzle and murk. Crickets chirped; geese honked as they headed south. The forest floor lost its snappy crispiness. After weeks of low grey skies, it was easy to forget the late summer heat, when it was a struggle to keep the gardens moist, to be ever vigilant for the fearful smell of smoke.

With the mining project threat having dissipated, the search for the author of the leaked envelopes became a favoured topic of discussion.

Derek lived his life at Linton's Beach much as he had before the accusations. Some scrubbing, with help from local volunteers, removed most of the graffiti from his truck, but the faint outline of the words remained indelible.

"It's not like the data is secret or hard to find if you know where to look. From what I understand, it was all from public or previously published documents," Derek said to Garba one morning as they sat in the café watching the whitecaps build up outside the bay.

Garba smiled. "Yeah, *if* you knew where to look, Derek. You and Dan did."

His grin said it all.

"Where is Dan, anyway?" she asked. "Haven't heard news of him or the *Serendipity* in a few weeks. He said he might check in..."

Before he left, she had shared several evenings on his boat, listening to the rain on the deckhouse roof. Eventually one of them would give a yawn and stretch. Garba would shrug into her authentic L.L. Bean oiled-canvas jacket, share a long hug, and duck through the hatchway into the black night.

Then Dan had cast off to go exploring, said he'd be back "in a while." Which was fine, but with the weather worsening, she had let her concern build.

She asked, "I know he doesn't have a cell phone... He laments what he calls 'the techno-tendrils of wireless' reaching deeper into the wilds. Do you know how to reach him? What about emergencies?"

"He's no reckless fool. The boat has a VHF radio and a satellite phone but he only turns it on when necessary. He called me a couple nights ago. Wanted to tell me again that he wasn't blaming anyone for the leak and his termination. Actually, he thought it was a pretty clever and bloodless way to win. He found a job up in the Broughton Archipelago as a winter caretaker in some rich man's fishing lodge. Claimed his cabin has more mod cons than any house on Pirate Island. He said twice to give you his number and call sign. To continue where your conversation left off. If you want."

She did.

EPHRAIM*

"Ya see them kids out front? More damned metal stuck through their ears an' lips than I got from the stinking Nazis at Dunkirk.

"An' look at their raggedy-ass clothes. Like something the bums wore riding the rail cars in the Depression.

"It's their parents' fault, y'know. I told my Larry that years ago. When he was running around in beads and growing long messy hair back in the sixties, calling himself Lawrence. I told him to smarten up. Now it's his kids that go around the village like some damned freaks. Not as bad as some, but still...

"Billy, another round for our table. Keep 'em coming."

The Royal Hotel was a drab two-storey building on the uphill side of Dunsmuir Street. Most of the upstairs windows were boarded over or covered with sun-bleached curtains so brittle they'd shatter if you tried to let sunlight into the cheap rooms. The papery husks of a thousand moths lay desiccated on the sills. The main floor pub's round tables were stained by spills and rings from innumerable beers,

---

*   "Old Ephraim" is a nineteenth-century term used in the American West to refer to grizzly bears (*Ursus arctos horribilis*). This is *not* the species in this story, but rather my own poetic licence.

burnt with shallow black canyons where cigarettes once lay forgotten by someone staggering off to the toilet or rising with fists up and chin down to settle a grievance. Stale smoke hung in sluggish layers. The first serious sou'easter of the season slammed into the windows with a wet slap.

Late autumn. The early frosts had come with the full moon. Taking their cue, the alder and maple leaves awaiting their final gust drooped from the branches. The hum of growth was winding down. In the hills around the village, the bears sniffed the crispness—deep memories rose in them as voracious hunger. It had been a dry summer: the berry crop was dismal and the salmon still waited for the rivers to rise. Food was scarce, so overcoming elemental fear, they ventured toward the village dump.

"Zip. Zero. There is absolutely nothing to do tonight. It sucks."

"Do you have to talk like that? I'm just trying..."

"Okay, sorry, Mom. Just all the guys are outta town with the rugby team, like no one's home. You going anywhere?"

"No, I have to get caught up with this online course. Then you can have the computer. For now, though, can you stop hovering?"

"Maybe I'll take the dog for a walk. Okay?"

She nodded and turned back to scowl at her laptop and the dining room table, which was layered in books and papers.

He flipped up the hood of his sweatshirt, whistled once and closed the back door. Their old dog hobbled down the steps. The squall had passed but burdened clouds scudded

EPHRAIM

overhead, barely restraining their wet load. Between them, stars winked through a well-scrubbed sky.

"An' another thing wrong with these kids. They got no respect for nothing. The other night I was coming home and a bunch of 'em were hanging round in front of the community hall. Think they'd move and let me, a veteran, get by? No damn way. Had to walk in the street. Got my shoes muddy. Flo gave me hell. Goddamn punks."

The convenience store lights buzzed and blinked in a rapid stutter. He paid for his Coke and stood looking at the magazine rack with a sigh. He'd dropped the dog home, but the rest of the evening still yawned ahead of him.

"Hey," a voice called from the other side of the rack. "What's up?"

"Jeez, am I glad to see you. I thought everyone was away. Whatcha doing?"

"Halloween's coming. And man, oh man, am I ready this year. My uncle just came up from Washington and stopped at some Indian reservation and bought a trunkload of fireworks. Stuff you can't get up here."

"Were you in on it last year?"

"No, I was on the mainland with my sister, but I saw it on TV. Looked awesome. You were there, eh?"

"Nah, my mom heard about it and kept me home. I don't think it was as bad as it looked. Some guys got loaded and fired a few Roman candles at the cop shop. But all the geezers got excited and next thing the fire department, even the Legion and the Mounties, were there and it all went crazy. Tear gas. More fireworks. Someone tossed a bench into the liquor store window, and then everyone ran away."

"You think *those* fireworks were something, come with me and see what I got stashed. This'll be the best Halloween yet."

Every afternoon, sitting comically on the hillside above the town dump, the bears watched the yellow machine crushing the trash bags, mattresses, old bikes, soggy sofas and delicious food scraps. At dusk, the man parked the compactor and drove off in a village truck. The bears waited, then moved down, following their long noses from all points of the compass, drawn like iron filings to a magnet. With careless glee, they ripped into the plastic bags and snurfled through the refuse. Prehensile tongues scoured inside cans, yellow claws dug and tore. Once sated, the bears retreated with stinking muzzles and paws to the forest and sleep. One or two remained alert, long necks swivelling and bobbing, awaiting messages of danger or opportunity.

"Last call, gentlemen. Early closing 'cause of the holiday tomorrow. Another beer?"

"Nah, I guess I better be heading home. The warden's probably waiting up for me anyhow, watching her soap operas or music shows... Well, maybe I got time for one more. Sure, gimme another."

A month earlier the village mayor, who also owned the hardware store, had sat with his council listening to the business at hand. More letters about the bears at the dump.

Some were from the usual greenies who were disgusted by the sight of these noble creatures eating Pampers. One was from a citizen who was out shooting rats—claimed he was chased and only escaped by the skin of his teeth. After much discussion, it was decided to erect a fence around the dump. Voted and passed. Council then retired across the street to the Royal.

Tossing back the last of his beer, a sleeve drawn across the mouth, he rose. "This time I gotta go. Gimme a half-dozen of them pickled eggs to take home. Hope them punks aren't still out there. When I was…" He waved goodbye to his cronies and lurched for the door.

"Starburst One Thousand. Sky Avenger. Crystal Fountain. Look at this one—a Super Sonic Air Bomb. This'll rattle the windows. Wanna try one now?"

"Yeah, let's go to the park. Your uncle is pretty cool to give you all these fireworks."

Stuffing their pyrotechnic loot into a plastic bag, the two boys came out of the alley beside the school and started down the main drag. A few cars rolled slowly by, a honk or wave directed at them. The rain still held off but the threat kept almost everyone indoors.

"Another Saturday night in Dullsville, eh? Well, this baby will wake things up."

"Got a lighter or some matches?"

"Crap, no. If I go home and ask Mom, she'll wanna know why. She's always afraid of me starting smoking, like her."

"There's someone coming out of the Royal. Ask him."

It had taken a few days for the workmen to erect the fence. Each night the bears came and sniffed the wire mesh, walked the length until they found where the men had stopped. But after three days it was done, and the bears walked around and around, sniffing and licking at the steel. The bigger ones stood up and pushed, but it held. With hunger rumbling in their bellies, they drifted toward town, toward garbage cans, orchards and compost bins.

"Huh, whaddya want?"

"Got a match, mister?"

"Yeah, my ass and your face! Ha, ha. Get a job, punk. Buy your own stuff."

"Just a match, y'old fart, no big deal."

"Get outta my way." He pushed past them and stumbled down the glistening sidewalk.

"What a jerk. Acting like that just for a freakin' match. Hey, what's that?" He pointed to the right angle of building and sidewalk. "We're in luck, it's a Bic. Someone must've fumbled it coming out of the Royal. Let's go do it!"

Night after night, the bears roamed the alleys and backyards. Dogs went insane, destroying doors to get let out and follow the scent of the black shadows, then clawing frantically to get back in. The bears sifted quietly through the village on soft pads, standing up now and then to peer over fences, even into the windows of the extended-care home on the hill. They became bolder and less fearful as they habituated to pizza scraps, rotting apples beneath the trees, anything left on a porch. Cats and smelly work boots disappeared.

The drizzle started again as the boys huddled under the picnic shelter. Carefully packing a firework into some sand, angling it out over the sports field, they lit the fuse. The trajectory of sparks traced a line through the squall then exploded in a huge fireball, cracking like thunder. Several lights went on in the houses around the park. The flash lit up the area like daylight. The boys blinked, eyes adjusting.

"Did you see that?"

"Where? What?"

"There, past the concession booth. By the dumpster. Something moved. Oh, jeez, there it is. It's a bear! It's coming this way, fast! Crap, let's get outta here."

The big animal had been ass-end up in the bin, sorting through the hot dog wrappers and soggy fries from the weekend's game. When the sparks streaked across the sky, she raised her snout to look, but the ensuing explosion blinded and panicked her. She dropped to the ground and took off running. Out of the park and up a nearby alley. Dazed and bewildered, she ricocheted off trash cans, sending them clattering down the hill, adding to her fright. Dogs erupted and doors flung open, sending noise and streaks of light into the night. The bear ran flat out, her shining fur rolling from one side to the other.

Taking a familiar shortcut home from the pub, the old man turned down an alley between the rows of houses. Belly full of beer, bag packed with pungent wrapped eggs, he reflected on his contentment.

"What the hell?" as the sky lit up in a massive explosion. "Them damned punks again." He continued down the gravel lane, muttering and condemning. Out of the black, wet night, something sootier than darkness came rushing toward him, skidded to a stop.

"Oh, sweet suffering Mary and Joseph, a bloody b-b-b..."

The bear stood to her full height, taller than the sputtering veteran, and swivelled her head around, smelling the acrid stench of pub smoke lingering on the man's plaid wool jacket. She had become less ruffled and made no move to back down. The bear sniffed loud and wet and rocked back and forth on her legs. Man and bear stood in the night, not moving, not taking their eyes off each other, not blinking. The clouds opened and soaked both, hiding the growing wet spot down the front of the man's dark trousers. Despite the downpour neither budged. She smelled the eggs and his yeasty beer breath. He stared at her black marble eyes and cursed quietly. The evening traffic had left the streets and time washed by, following the gutter water with its cargo of butts, papers and brown leaves.

"Jeez, that was a huge bang!" the boy panted from the safety of his front porch. "That bear scared the crap outta me. Wanna go find it?"

"Yeah, sure. Let's take another bomb. For protection."

He was starting to shiver now. The adrenalin had subsided and his raspy breath slowed. He raised the arm holding the egg bag. The motion elicited a deep growl and a toothy snarl that stood his neck stubble on end. Down came the arm, the black beady eyes following his every move. The bear dropped to all fours and edged closer, lips still curled back. Within arm's reach now, she stood again.

"Oh, Flo, I love you..." he said spontaneously.

EPHRAIM

They remained locked in a first-one-to-blink staring contest, noses inches apart, neither moving.

Armed with a Screecher and youthful bravado, the boys hugged close to buildings and porches, keeping the fuse dry. Travelling through the alleys and streets they knew so well, they came upon the tableau of man and bear.

"It's him, it's the mean ol' guy. *And* the bear."

"We gotta do something..." The boy fumbled for the green plastic lighter. Aiming the firework across the street, he lit the fuse.

"Hey, mister. Run!"

The trajectory of sparks and payload bounced twice on the wet pavement and exploded with a window-rattling bang. The bear panicked, ejected a smelly splatter of berry and garbage poop, charged past the shivering man, knocking him over with a heavy shoulder, and somehow in her fright remembered to dexterously grab the egg bag in her mouth as she bolted for the sanctuary of the forest. Ears ringing, she glanced back but kept running with that rolypoly gait. The old man sat numbly on the blue-black pile of excrement, mouth opening and closing but no words coming out.

He reached in his jacket for a pack of smokes, picked one out with a shaking hand and began patting himself down for a light. Unsuccessful, he looked up at the kids.

"Gotta match?"

The boys looked at each other with a grin. "Yeah, my..." The old man, wet, shaking, piss-stained and sitting in reeking bear crap, waited for the rest of the sentence: "...my pleasure. Here, lemme help you up."

BY THE BOOK

The door is off the plane, making it easier to see the mountainside swirling with flames below the wheels as we claw for altitude. At a hundred and forty knots the thunder of the engines and the buffeting wind swirls into the crowded cabin. We communicate with hand signals, mouthed syllables, eye contact. The Twin Otter drones on with its burden of jumpers and fire tools: pumps, hoses, shovels, Pulaskis and crates of Gatorade. I sit back against the bulkhead and try to get as comfortable as my unwieldy gear will allow. I squirm under my harness but can't move too much. Keep the load balanced. This is my fifth season and I know the procedures. But cocky is dangerous so I count the rivets on the back of the pilot's seat. One, two, three, four, five... The rookies stare blankly, running through the sequence of what is about to happen so there are no surprises, no glitches.

"Upon leaving the aircraft, start the count, cross your arms snug over your chest, elbows in, good tight L bend at the hips with your legs together, don't look down, stare at the horizon. Remain stable," preached the instructors, "or you may well perish. Knees to the breeze, boys."

"You're going back again, aren't you?" Shari asked him from where she was stretching on the living room floor. It was a fair enough question, but Brad had to dance around the response. It was April and the snow was melting, exposing all the winter's detritus: dog turds, beer cans and whisky bottles, some kid's rusty bike, yard tools surprised by early snow and left to corrode, and the set of truck keys he dropped while juggling the doorknob, an armful of grocery bags and two flats of Lucky. Spring thaw, everything rushing west, the whole world tilting, rumpled mountain ranges shedding avalanches like a dog's scruffy winter pelt.

"It's a good job. Initial Attack crew leader again this year. Running my own team."

"Where are you applying?"

He listed the five or six bases where he sent his resumé and application. None were anywhere near a town or city; such was the nature of the business.

"If it's like last year, it won't really matter where you're stationed, will it? I mean, I'd be spending a lot of time alone in a trailer. Again. Just trying to stay as close to your camp as possible. But even so, I think I saw you a total of nine days the whole season. And when you were home, you needed downtime."

"Yeah, but you have me all winter."

"Feast or famine, eh?"

It was like that. Never home, then in each other's hair day and night through the long months of snow and dark—a pressure test for any relationship. He tried to find work, but who would hire a guy who is going to scamper come spring? Day labour jobs on construction sites and the call board for the railway were preferable to flipping burgers or mopping floors in the school. Shari taught yoga classes all winter in the basement of their rented house. Walking back lanes in his idleness, he found several pieces of carpet and underlay to make a welcoming surface for her students. It looked like a patchwork quilt: a square of wool weave, some godawful orange shag, striped stair runners, and an oval of handmade braided rug, all held together with the wonder of duct tape.

...six, seven, eight, nine. One missing. Ten. The plane bucks and shudders as a fist of heat punches up from the fire roaring through the landscape of dead pine below us. I grin at Kenny, my number two. He gives me a thumbs up. The jumpmaster is on the floor with his head out the door looking for the drop zone. The plane banks a big circle and flattens its climb. Over the bobbing helmets of my crew, the pilot's hand moves up to the overhead throttles. The two rumbling Pratt & Whitney engines idle back. The jumpmaster tosses out a weighted ribbon to gauge the wind drift and talks to the pilot through his helmet mic. Another turn into the wind and the steady yellow light goes on. Get ready. Final buddy check. Make sure the locking pins are removed from our canopy packs. All snaps and backups secured. D-handle for the emergency chute slipped from its Velcro safety cover and, God forbid, ready for use.

Why are my teeth clenched? My logbook in the locker back at the base is full of my perfect jumps, five years with no accidents. Still, I grind my molars and stare at the trainee in my team. He looks up and shows me a nervous smile.

As we tilt into another turn, the plane bounces hard on a thermal speed bump. We float weightless for a spell, and then slam down solid on the aluminum floor. Nausea clamours for attention but I discourage it by taking a hard swallow. With a yank, I tighten the chest strap on my jump harness, hoping that will keep the pancakes down.

"How many more summers do you have left in your back and knees, Brad? It's one thing to be a hotshot smokejumper in your late twenties, but what happens when you..."

"Grow up? That again, Shari? You think I'm just playing around on fire control? Playing with man toys like helicopters and pumps and big machines? Come on, I'm not Peter Pan in Neverland. A couple more seasons, that's all. I mean, it gets into your blood, wildfire."

"Oh, I know. It's this all-or-nothing lifestyle. Either you are housebound, staring at the calendar, counting the days, or you're gone. I'm just looking for some balance here. You go off on these big project fires for weeks and I don't hear from you..."

"Radio silence, babe. You know we can't talk about the fires over the air."

"Oh, for God's sake, Brad. I don't care about the fires. I want to hear from *you*. A simple phone call now and then surely won't endanger your crew and the precious reputation of the Forest Service."

"Forty-seven kilometres. That's how far it was to the nearest phone last season. No cell coverage, no nothing. I missed you too; I wanted to hear your voice, but..."

"Balance. That's all I want. You and some balance, my lover boy." She assumed the Half Lord of the Fishes Pose, Ardha Matsyendrasana, twisting her body in a position he had never achieved despite his robust build. Strength had little to do with it.

The yellow light starts blinking and the jumpmaster catches my eye, points to me and raises two fingers. My crew goes second. The first jumpers get into position, lining up in a bent-over shuffle toward the door. Funny how no one looks at anybody else's eyes on final approach. We make morbid jokes on the ground, but in the air it's all business, no fucking around tolerated. There is a time and place for that later.

The blinking light goes off and the red one comes on. The first jumper is in the doorway, boot braced against the slipstream, hands clenched on either side of the exit. The Otter wiggles across the sky, the pilot fighting the angry, roiling air. Our foe awaits below. Even three thousand feet up, we taste her hot, sweet breath and she knows we're coming after her. The jumpmaster slaps the leg of the first man and he throws himself into the wind. The next three shuffle and grab sky. We follow. I put the rookie in the number one spot. Best to get it over with quickly. This is the place to learn faith.

Growing up on the prairie, far from these flaming hills, I thought faith was found in the limestone church we attended every Sunday morning and Wednesday evening for bible study. Faith that my dog would still be at home when I returned, faith that Mom would unfailingly put a meal on the table exactly at eight, twelve and six o'clock, faith that Dad would bring home another model airplane kit from his latest road trip.

I shuffle into position behind the rookie and think about what really counts: having complete and utter faith in your gear.

"Okay. Let's make a deal." She stood up with an effortless grace and leaned forward with her elbows on the dining room table. "Two more summers, then we'll..."

"Is that two after this one or two counting this one?"

"Oh, Brad, don't make fun of me, that doesn't help and it really pisses me off. Maybe this *is* the second year. Maybe last year was the first. You know how crazy you were last winter here in Revelstoke. Two days a week with the CPR chipping ice off the track. Lots of future there."

Brad nodded, remembering getting up in the freezing dark, long before a sulky dawn, pulling on layers of polypro, wool and heavy canvas coveralls that kept the cold out, at least until midday. The deep valleys lay frozen in the heavy shadow of the mountains; the sun wouldn't be warming the track until late April. Until then, Brad and a few others rose early to clean the chunks of icy dirt and rock from the switches and signal plates. They carried crude, heavy tools and propane tiger torches to melt the hard chunks from the brittle steel.

"So, if I was to quit fire..."

"Not *if*, Brad. When."

So, what's my choice? he thought, looking at Shari. They had been together six years and had shared interests: hiking, skiing, mountain biking and cooking. The latter provided many evenings' entertainment through the short days and dim early nights. Preparing a meal from a new recipe sometimes deteriorated into a rowdy food fight, with batter or filling spattered around the kitchen. Brad grabbing a towel and wiping off Shari's shirt, unbuttoning it to get at the smears, then forgetting the clean-up as other matters took over.

"I just finished reading this book about factory farms," Shari said. "I don't want to live someplace where I have to buy dead meat from tortured animals. I want a big garden and chickens. Maybe goats. I want a home, Brad. Not just a winter refuge. Not just a summer trailer, no matter how magnificent the view." She often lay awake, thinking about what was, is, or could be, while Brad snored beside her. She envied his ability to roll over and sleep; to not replay the unsettling events of the day like a loop of film, the same conversations over and over again. There was nothing she could share with him, because he would tell her how to fix it even if that was not her question. He'd laugh at her trouble and tell her what to do, like he approached the fire line. This isn't working so simply do this. Don't lie awake staring at the water-stained ceiling.

"Honestly, I just want to feel like I live where I belong, and belong where I live."

The rookie crouches in the doorway waiting for the slap. I stand directly behind him, ready to nudge if need be. No matter how much training, how many drills and practices, the first operational jump is a scary bugger. Maybe it is looking down into the columns of smoke and flames licking high into the thin mountain air, even from this altitude feeling the heat on your face, searching for a hole in the forest cover and not finding one. Tree landings are hard on the body despite the Kevlar suit, the helmet with its face screen, the padded high collar, and the reinforced crotch ("keep your legs crossed when you hit the branches, boys... think of your future family..."). I remember my first jump. A good, steady exit, the bright canopy billowing in textbook fashion, I spotted an opening and pulled the steering toggles to drive my chute toward it. But it was no flower-strewn alpine meadow of postcard beauty. My boots punched through the foot of sphagnum moss covering a marsh and I found myself up to my waist in cold tannic blackwater with my chute and lines collapsing over me. I earned the nickname "Swampy."

Feet first into the unknown. Faith that the static line attached to the plane will deploy my chute on time. Faith that Shari will be there when I get off. Not like Kenny, who found a note stuck to the door of his house when he got back from a long and stubborn smoke in Fort Nelson.

Each time Brad left, she went through a regime of parting. The first few days, she walked around the house, sifting through his immediate detritus. A few pieces of errant clothing under the bed. Lifting his favourite coffee mug to her lips hoping to catch a taste of him. Walking into a room half expecting to see him on the couch and surprised when he is not. Once a week passed she began to feel a strange hunger. Her desire caused him to appear in the heat of the Kootenay summer, to float shimmering on the dusty road past their parked trailer. When she and the yellow dog went riding the trails, his shadow followed them because she so willed it. But after a few more days, even these ghosts evaporated, and she was left with a lonely but oddly welcome sense of simplicity. The bed was all hers; no hot body to roll away from on the still August nights, no one to explain everything to. But no one when the night wind moaned or when the redneck neighbour came around too often.

The rookie gets the slap and tumbles out. I grab the door frame with both hands and hurl myself after him. Assume the position, start the count, don't think, play by the book. *Jump— thousand, wait—thousand, set—thousand* and on cue the umbilical static line pulls the pack pins, the spring-loaded pilot chute fires out and I feel the drag pull me vertical in my snug harness. *Look—thousand.* Tilting my head back, I watch the deployment sleeve slip off and release the main canopy—the big, beautiful square of brilliant red and white. After all the noise of the Twin Otter, after the roar of the wind and the metallic taste of fear as I started falling through the sky—now comes the silence. Below me the rookie whoops under his canopy and I shout back and start laughing.

Forgotten is the gruelling work that awaits us below, digging fire line, dragging hoses, felling burning snags, breathing smoke and ash. I float above the flames. For precious moments I am an equal to Daedalus, wiser than Icarus, smarter than King Minos. Borne on nylon wings, looking to the great ranges and ramparts stretching north to south, away to hazy nothings. Monashee, Selkirk and Purcell. Brother to eagles. Ecstasy.

Shari sits on the step of the swaybacked trailer bent by years of winter snowpack; the floor so uneven they had to shim everything. Brad meticulously cut a wafer off each of the chair legs so they would sit level around the table, but they had to mark on the floor exactly where every leg was to go or they'd wobble precariously. No balance there.

The yellow dog raises his muzzle and watches her stand, go into the house and return with a pad of paper and a pencil. She makes two columns on the page: his and hers. Chewing on the pencil, she stares across the yard at the lodgepole pine, dead from the beetle infestation. Dead like the millions of others turning the forest into a tinderbox. His list: Wildfire Control, dark beer, old movies, Wild, Fire, Control, yellow dog, skiing, restless. Hers: what was on top? Five acres, independence, award-winning novels, pasta, him, snow tires, babies.

Babies? She was content with her own company, willingly residing in her body. Perhaps yoga helped. Brad craved having people around, loved to be involved in everything on all sides of him, sometimes micromanaging the whole scene to a maddening degree. Crew boss mentality—hard to turn off. She knew that. In winter there were long evenings when no one came by; nothing on the crummy TV, snow too deep or furious to venture outside. Brad paced five steps one way, then the other, in the small living room. Shari curled up in a chair with a book, avoiding eye contact. Winter brought out the necessity of unsatisfactory compromises, of turbulent conversations when words fizzled and were picked up later, still smouldering. She often slept on the lumpy couch. After a few weeks, irritations sifted in like the snow in the corners of the ill-fitting windows.

Babies? She imagined what that would be like in winter if Brad kept up what she thought was his first love—firefighting. Stuck in some rental with diapers hanging from makeshift clotheslines, windows steamed up with domestic funk. And would summers be any better? None of the women attached to other smokejumpers had babies. Shari had a hard time making friends anyhow. She relied on Brad's ebullient personality to open doors, maintain conversations, introduce her to others. She loved his elegance and poise. She loved *him*.

By now the lists were filling the page. Shari looked at them and began crossing off the ones that cancelled each other like she was doing high school algebra equations, pluses and minuses. When the sheet was mostly marred with x's and lines through words, she stared at what was left, swore quietly under her breath, wadded it into a ball and threw it into the yard. Yellow dog ran out and brought it back, thinking it fun. His black gums drooling in a happy grin, tail thumping on the dry earth.

"This is no game, boy. This is some hard shit."

In spite of her words she couldn't help laughing at the dog's simple allegiance. She looked up at the clear blue mountain sky and caught the ever-present scent of smoke.

Play by the book. Fall stable, have faith, seek balance.

THE BEAST WITHIN

Water has three forms: liquid, ice and vapour. Mixed they are slush, like quicksand, having no edges, no hardness, offering only passive resistance.

Abel always thought it'd happen to the other guy. Not him. Now it had. The last roll of the dice, the flip of a card. He never thought his days would end like this, fallen into a freezing ditch and soaked up to his hips. It had snowed for three days and then, as so often happens on the Island, it rained.

The more he flailed, the tighter the clamp around his soggy pants, his legs already aching from the cold. Sunk into a ditch he had dug, a roadside trench that cut across the sidehill of their family woodlot. It was getting dark and he couldn't feel his feet. Teeth chattering. Shivering. A mammal's final response.

A flock of chickadees flitted through the thick conifer branches looking for a last evening meal from their day's stash of seeds and buds. They cocked their black-capped heads and watched Abel with bright, curious eyes. He watched them ruffle themselves into feathery footballs for the night.

Cozy, he thought. Wish I was one.

He knew his situation was dire but his brain seemed to be observing his dilemma from far away—detached and unable to act. He looked down at his own legs as if they belonged elsewhere, the ability to move forgotten. Thoughts hovered, then fled unheeded.

Several years before, a similar rain-on-snow event occurred but he had stayed home by the warm fire and only glanced out the window at the gloomy afternoon, thinking all was well. The next day he drove his truck up to the woodlot behind their rural home. Around a corner, the road was missing. A deeply eroded gully full of dirty rushing water and tumbling stones poured down the grade. He grabbed a shovel and struggled up what was left of Branch West 120 until he found a clogged culvert diverting meltwater out of the ditch, sluicing tons of rocks and gravel down the slope. He scooped out the plug of mud, branches and creeping blackberry, thinking about calling Howie and his bulldozer to push the gravel back uphill.

A low beam of weak late winter sunshine slanted through the smooth glistening trunks of the young forest of fir and chalky alder, focusing on a solitary crystalline prism of pendent snow with enough meagre heat to release a single drop. The water did what water does. It fell into a palm-sized pool, then tumbled in a giggling trickle to become a rivulet, gaining direction and purpose. Others joined in a wildly playful release to form a stream following the path of least resistance, its headlong rush to the great awaiting saltchuck.

He deepened his ditches to hasten their descent.

Abel had leaned on the shovel and thought he had been a fool to ignore the weather signs and promised never again. He finished chastising himself and looked up at the young forest around him. He had planted a hundred trees for each child and grandchild born. He remembered the April before, when the musty smell of awakening forest duff rose from the hole he had dug. His granddaughter carefully nestled a seedling and tamped soil around the hair-thin, cinnamon-coloured roots. When the bucket was empty, they found a log in the sun and unwrapped apple slices and leftover chicken drumsticks. They ate quietly, only talking to point out magnificent discoveries.

Now the kids and their kids were gone, far afield, making their own ways in life. The trees grew tall, straight, strong, and he was an old man with gimpy legs and a thick folder from his doctor, who had told him it was time to take it easy. But pride is a hard burden to unload. Try as he might, Abel thought that laying it down was not worth the effort.

"Isn't it enough just to know in your heart that you've done the best you could. Why make a fuss?"

He tried to explain: "I've spent fifty of my seventy years in the West Coast forests in a place where value is measured in output, in grit, in the ability to stand out in the raging gale, drenched to the skin, on the bounce dodging hazards of every description—vegetal, animal, human or mechanical—and not give in. Don't get me wrong, I'm not trying to sound macho or heroic. And I wouldn't have any other history."

But after all these rough-and-tumble years doing what he loved, his body began to fail. He knew why but shrugged when the doctor asked. Careless acts are not made less so by disclosing them.

He had been falling trees on a pole contract, taking only the selected ones: pipestem straight with few branches and no defects such as catfaces, scrapes or fungi.

Concentrating on making his saw cuts true to aim, he didn't notice a twelve-metre hemlock snag, dead from root rot, beginning to loosen and fall from the impacts of his previous trees hitting the ground. Something or someone made him turn his head and twist his body around so the tree came down across his shoulders, not his head, and glanced off his back, driving him to the ground and pinning him there. He fumbled for his metal safety whistle and blew six times for help.

He took a week off and was left with a shiny blue tattoo where the skin had been flayed, but he was grateful to be alive, thanks to that unseen something or someone that made him look up at the last minute. The corner of his eye was a busy place, like an old-time movie—images flickering, as transient as a spring cloud's scoot. Sometimes he heard voices, like echoes off a rock face across a lily-pad lake. Was that it?

Since that day, backache was a constant reminder. And the X-ray confirmed it.

He figured something was wrong when the technician holding the print looked at it, gasped "Holy cow," and called for the doctor.

It revealed a spine that resembled a train derailment. One vertebra was jammed into the next in painful misalignment, all grinding away at his quivering nerves. He was admitted for spinal decompression surgery.

He followed the post-surgery exercises as best he could, and for a month he healed, stretched and moved gingerly. Then the physiotherapist noticed Abel's right leg wasn't responding like it should. Yes, the leg was dragging behind the rest of his body, like the Newfoundland time zone, half an hour off the other Atlantic provinces. First it was just the one, then the other too.

It was like they had lost their wires to the brain, and his brain forgot it was connected to a pair of legs. Each and every step or movement now required forethought. He had to tell one foot to move, then the other. A short walk to get the mail was exhausting and hardly worth it. Usually only flyers or requests for money.

The physio had quietly mentioned other symptoms of Parkinson's disease and tests verified it. An affliction that screws and bolts wouldn't fix. Like some ravening beast within his own body, uninvited and unwelcome.

For the next few years, Abel stumbled and gimped, avoiding the scrutiny of the masses where possible. Their curious eyes slid from his face to the dull leg and shuffling foot. He often felt like a vole, frozen in fear by the unblinking stare of the predator looking for the halt and lame. Centre ring at the freak show. Like having a public affliction, this stooped posture, this limping walk. Always the irritating questions, always the need to share their unwelcome advice and experiences, always with the unspoken "There but for the grace of God…"

Never much for going to town once he quit drinking at the hotel, but a shopping list gave him a reason. After groceries, a box of galvanized nails and, watching for errant pedestrians and cyclists who thought the road was theirs alone, he decided he had earned a reward. He lurched out of his truck, aiming at Starbucks for a ridiculously priced coffee, but caught his scuffling toe on the curb and fell flat on his face. The hipsters with their man buns and beard beads rushed up and asked, "Hey, bro, you okay?" As if lying in a pool of blood was normal. As if, despite his years, they still made him out as a "bro."

Abel later admitted he enjoyed all the attention from the pretty ladies, but he failed to convince them that once the bleeding slowed and the world stopped whirling, he'd be just fine to drive home if they'd help him into his truck.

"Can I call someone for a ride? Can your wife come and pick you up?" asked one of the crowd, noticing Abel's worn wedding band. Making an assumption.

"I doubt it. Sonja died two years ago."

Abel returned to his farm. Food had lost any appeal and with no one else to cook for he had become gaunt. After punching the last holes in his belt, worn bib overalls clothed him. He made his regular morning porridge in the same pot he used to heat his noontime soup, then his supper of canned stew on even numbered days, mac and cheese on odd. One pan, one bowl, one spoon. Facing one empty chair across the chipped yellow kitchen table.

He sought familiar routines and places for reassurance and solace, tried to find comfort in night sounds: the hum of the fridge, the tick of the wall clock, woodstove crackling. His old dog, Blink, his last best friend, lay jerking, snoring and flapping black lips in dreams of his own youthful antics.

The big black Lab, now with a greying muzzle, was named for how quickly he'd disappear into the night for his hours-long prowls, raiding the neighbour's garbage cans and patrolling his turf. Abel often feared he'd never return. Would the wolves corner him, or a cougar he treed tire of her awkward refuge and descend on Blink, calling his bluff? On pitch-dark nights, with rain and wind howling in on sou-easters up the Strait, Abel would listen for a scratch on the door. There'd be Blink, soaked to the bone, tongue lolling out from a satisfied feral grin. Relieved, Abel would dry him as he made several circles on his blanket by the woodstove before clunking down with a deep sigh.

Time became like dark amber maple syrup. He moved slowly for someone once used to stepping over all obstacles.

He walked in halting steps to his shop in the back of the barn, where he sat on a stained dining room chair and stared at his blotched hands, knuckles like dry walnuts, palms with geologically deep cracks, then raised his face to look around the room.

Wooden apple crates from the Okanagan, dove-tail-cornered ammunition boxes, a dozen shovels of every size and shape, the heavy Jack-all, a peavey, ropes, chains and a come-along, cardboard boxes of plumbing and electrical leftovers, cans of bolts and nuts, metal tool boxes full of wrenches, pliers and socket sets, sacks of birdseed for winter's visitors. A Christmas tree stand from when the farmhouse was filled with family. Used nails to straighten out on a rainy day. Like today. On a spike driven into a beam hung a weight of power saw chains, sharpened down to a nub for saws he no longer had or could use.

A shower pattered on the tin roof; the wind rattled the loose-fitting window he never got around to nailing tight. So many things left undone. Now with the beast within, he wondered if he ever would. What was it he did yesterday that took him all day to do?

Abel tore off the last page of his calendar. Forty centimetres of heavy snow had fallen in three days. Then it rained. Trees in the woodlot cracked under the load. The snow settled but was still deep. The feeder was busy with the jaunty chickadees, juncos and raucous jays.

His preferences were trees, dogs and some, but not all, blood relatives. This beloved forest was his sanctuary. Even with the beast erasing cogent thought, the bush was familiar yet still renewing. Every visit gave a new sight or sound. Expecting the same welcome, he drove as far as the snowy road remained passable, then slewed the truck around. Years in the bush ingrained the habit of turning it facing out in case of the need for a speedy exit. Some things he remembered.

He left the truck and slogged up the hillside road, ensuring that the culverts and ditches were flowing free with the huge volume of runoff. Impatient water gurgled beneath the sagging snow.

He took just two steps off the road and suddenly sank up to his knees in icy slush that quickly saturated his woollen pants. Already wobbly and sweaty from the effort of walking, he was now firmly gripped. Slush, like fine cold silt, clamped around both boots. He realized he had maybe ten minutes before hypothermia would overcome him.

He twisted around to look at the sanctuary of his truck. It looked as distant as his home bed. Cab light was on, and he saw Blink's head silhouetted as he whined and paced back and forth in the cab watching him struggle. And sink.

As the dusk shadows lengthened, an evening breeze moved the snow-laden branches, dumping more snow on his head and back. He envied the black-capped chickadees that had taken shelter in the dense fir boughs, bunched together through the long, dark night.

I'm done for, he thought. Hope the dog gets found soon. Don't want him to pee in my truck.

Then he heard something or someone moving through the darkening forest, a big something. With a snapping of dry lower branches, spraying a scattering of fresh snow shaken from its crown, a laden fir snag fell across the ditch just in front of him. The disturbed chickadees exploded scolding out of the roost tree and disappeared into the forest.

Abel stared at the log for a minute, not immediately recognizing the opportunity. But the shiny scar on his back had its own memory. He reached out his sodden arms and grabbed the snag with dull fingers. The talons of the beast released and his boots came free.

With caution he began to wallow himself out of the ditch. On the road, he tried to rise from his hands and knees, only to collapse. But each struggle brought him closer to the Ford.

After what felt like a lifetime, he opened the door and pulled himself in. Blink looked up and licked life into Abel's blue fingers as they grasped the steering wheel. Another bush trick: leave the keys in the ignition. No fumbling. The engine started immediately and blessedly warm air sighed from the vents.

In a few minutes, the foggy windshield cleared and as he dropped into first gear four-wheel drive, he glanced in the rear-view mirror and saw the lifesaving broken snag lying at an angle over the desperately trampled snow around the ditch.

"What do you think, old Blink?"

The dog perked up his ears, made a couple of circuits, shook his head, spraying Lab slobber around the seat, then dove down to lick himself.

Something. Someone.

ACKNOWLEDGEMENTS

Many have encouraged and guided me in the construction, writing, editing; polishing my rambling syntax and crude sentence structures. Editors Trevor McMonagle and Pam Robertson kindly suggested to "drown my kittens," along with the help of copy editor Caroline Skelton and proofreader David Marsh. Sentences were strengthened by the change of a punctuation mark, or deletion of one of my superfluous clever phrases. Many others helped to bring this book into the world, including Libris Simas Ferraz and Carleton Wilson, who designed it, and Anna Comfort O'Keeffe.

Dave Young saved me from the gremlins of cyberspace when my clumsy fingers hit the wrong keys, erasing a day's work. Howard White at Harbour Publishing provided me with the belief I had something to share.

And to my First Reader and wife, Judy, I owe you morning coffee for years.

Finally a tip of the hard hat to all the loggers, hippies, stump farmers and scoundrels whose lives have often been the grit in the oyster.

ABOUT THE AUTHOR

Harold Macy is the author of *The Four Storey Forest* (Poplar Publishing, 2011) and *San Josef* (Tidewater Books, 2020) and has been published in various literary journals. He has worked for the BC Forest Service Research Branch, been a silviculture contractor for a local forestry company, fought wildfires, had rain in his lunch pail heli-logging up in the mid-coast inlets, and for many years was the forester at the UBC Oyster River Research Farm, where he wrote and delivered courses in small-scale forestry and agroforestry.